Souls Entwined

SOUL PURPOSE

NICHELLE GREGORY

Soul Purpose
ISBN # 978-1-78430-669-4
©Copyright Nichelle Gregory 2015
Cover Art by Posh Gosh ©Copyright June 2015
Interior text design by Claire Siemaszkiewicz
Totally Bound Publishing

Published in 2015 by Totally Bound Publishing, Newland House, The Point, Weaver Road, Lincoln, LN6 3QN, United Kingdom.

Totally Bound Publishing is a subsidiary of Totally Entwined Group Limited.

SOUL PURPOSE

Dedication

In this life, darkness touches us all and it's often through the cracks that we truly appreciate the light pouring in.

Special thanks to Nicki for giving me something other than heartbreak to focus on.

Chapter One

Shannon glanced out of the window of her limo at the bright lights of the city and the people enjoying the nightlife in Las Vegas. For the next few weeks, Sin City would be her home. Shannon opened her gold clutch and took out her compact. She checked her appearance, pleased with her smoky eye makeup. It was the perfect complement to her sequined halter cocktail dress. Shannon turned her face from side to side, smoothing back an errant ginger strand into the elegant bun she'd fashioned. She blew out a breath, admiring the way the sparkling square-cut diamond studs in her ears caught the light. "You're bloody ready for this."

Shannon put away her mirror, knowing she at least looked ready for the evening ahead as Clyde, her driver, opened her door. She took Clyde's offered hand, got out of the vehicle and smiled for the flash of camera going off.

"I was instructed to bring you to the back entrance in order to avoid some fans that got wind of tonight's party, but we didn't avoid all of the press."

"It's okay, Clyde. Thank you."

Clyde tilted his head in her direction. "My pleasure, Ms. Erby. I hope you enjoy yourself tonight."

"I do too."

Clyde grinned. "Just call me and I'll pull the car around for you when you're ready to go."

"All right. Will do." Shannon thanked him again before acknowledging the doorman waiting for her. She stepped up onto the curb, surprised by the few unexpected butterflies taking flight in her stomach.

Shannon pivoted in her stilettos, aware of both men watching her as she entered the Banner Hotel. The opulence of the building was evident even in the narrow hallway. Shannon tore her gaze off the tiered chandelier hanging over head, annoyed by the curious case of jitters threatening her normal cool. Her heels clicked on the marble floor, blending in her ears with the erratic beat of her heart. "Ridiculous."

Shannon straightened her spine and tightened her grip on her little sequined purse, rethinking her decision to attend this gathering alone. Going to a party without a date wasn't usually an issue for her but tonight she was nervous. This was her official debut with the cast and crew of *Celeb Hotel Chef* as a producer and host.

Correction, *co-host*.

Shannon bit the inside of her lip to keep from cursing Shawn Rill. She'd been under the impression she'd be hosting the show solo when she and Shawn hadn't been able to agree on a suitable anchor to join her. Although initially having a co-host had seemed like a great suggestion, Shannon had been secretly relived. She had never truly relished the idea of sharing the spotlight with anyone once the cameras got rolling, but Shawn had made an executive decision. He had selected Ryder Stevens as her co-host…a decision he'd left her in the dark about until this morning. "Damn him."

Shannon would meet Ryder for the first time tonight. Despite her irritation, she understood why Shawn had given the job to Ryder. With an impressive background as a music producer, he was a rising star in television after becoming a judge for a popular talent show. Audiences loved to tune in to see what Ryder would say. He was known for his dashing good looks, his silver tongue and his family's wealth, thanks to his father's wise investments in several Internet start-up companies.

Shannon stifled a yawn, uncharacteristically tired as she approached the doors leading into Tempted, the hotel's five-star restaurant. She hoped Ryder wasn't as egotistical in person as he was on that show she'd seen him on. Like it or not, the two of them needed a good rapport once they started filming. The job, albeit a short-term gig, would be a lot easier if she didn't have to fake chemistry for the sake of ratings.

"Shannon."

Shannon turned her head and saw Aimee and her husband walking toward her. "Hello, you two." She gave Aimee a quick hug then shook Kaden's hand. "I see you were able to convince your husband to join you."

"I didn't have to twist his arm." Aimee gazed up at Kaden, her love for him shining in her eyes. "We had such a blast the last time we were here. We couldn't wait to come back for the premiere of the show. I convinced a friend to join us too."

Shannon smiled. "How nice. Vegas is great escape from the mundane."

"That it is." Kaden slipped his arm around Aimee's waist. "My wife told me she enjoys getting a chance to wear dresses she's had stashed in the back of the closet for years and *I* love seeing her in them."

"Well"—Shannon touched Aimee's shimmering tangerine dress—"keeping this in the back of your closet should be a crime. You both look fantastic."

"Look who's talking." Aimee gestured at Shannon's attire. "You are *stunning* in that little number." Aimee shook her head. "I don't know how you walk in those stilettos."

Shannon chuckled. "I don't plan to do too much walking tonight. Have you two been inside already?"

"We just got here." Kaden rubbed his stomach. "I can't wait to sample this world-class cuisine."

"You're in for a treat." Shannon's pulse increased when she saw how crowded it was inside the fancy restaurant.

"We were trying to wait for my girlfriend but she's taking too long." Aimee checked her phone. "We decided to come down, grab a table and get this party started. Oh, here comes Ava now."

Shannon turned her head to see a pretty Latina woman approaching.

"*Hola, amigos.*" Ava let out a tiny squeal. "It's so nice to meet you, Ms. Erby. You rocked as host for *Celeb Chef.*"

"Thanks. It's very nice to meet you too, and please, call me Shannon." Shannon smiled warmly at Ava, admiring the way the strapless dark rose evening gown she wore hugged all her curves.

"This is so exciting!" Ava glanced around then frowned. "There are so many cameras around. How do you get used to it, Shannon?"

"After a while you forget they're there, but it does get tiring. I live for my comfy moments at home out of the eye of the public."

Ava nodded. "I bet."

"Are we ready to go in, ladies?" Kaden gestured toward the lit entrance of Tempted.

"Oh, yeah. Let's go in and celebrate. We're in Vegas baby! Whoo ooo!" Ava waved her sleek black clutch as they laughed. "There are several drinks with my name written all over them."

"Speaking of drinks" — Aimee placed her hand on Shannon's arm as they walked — "we must share a toast to celebrate our joint efforts to make *Celeb Hotel Chef* a success."

"We most definitely will." Shannon followed them into the swanky space, scanning the well-dressed crowd. She caught sight of Shawn talking to one of the female contestants for the show and returned his wave. "I suppose I must make my rounds."

"Right. I have a few people I need to chat with too." Aimee giggled when Kaden squeezed her closer to his side. "Have fun. We'll all catch up later."

"Brilliant." Shannon observed the lovey couple as they walked off, laughing with Ava. She liked the way the two interacted with one another.

"I see you haven't had your first glass of champagne."

Shannon turned to look at Shawn then smiled. "Not yet." She reached for the flute he offered her. "Thanks."

"You're welcome." Shawn took a drink from his glass as he eyed her from head to toe. "Man, that's a helluva dress. I think you should wear it on the show."

Shannon forced another polite grin. "I just might." She raised her glass, tasted the bubbly drink and prayed the alcohol would quickly soothe her nerves. "So, where is my new co-host?"

"Running late." Shawn cocked his head as he studied her. "You okay with my choice?"

It was a cursory question. Shannon was fully aware Shawn couldn't care less what she thought about his decision to cast Ryder. "Ryder has a legion of fans, I'm sure he'll increase viewership for *Celeb Hotel Chef*."

Shawn nodded. "My thoughts exactly. Ryder's got just the kind of energy we need." He nodded his head to whomever approached from behind her. "Speak of the devil…"

Shannon glanced over her shoulder and saw Ryder coming toward them. He stood out, handsome and tall, and he made a striking figure in his tailored charcoal suit.

"I know you probably had some reservations about me selecting Ryder but I'm certain the chemistry between you two on screen is going to be golden." Shawn placed his empty flute on the tray of a server passing by then grabbed another. "I can't wait to introduce you guys."

Shannon nodded, unsure of how to respond. She heard Ryder laugh as he stopped to greet a few people. Their gazes met and she offered a small grin, which he returned with a mega-watt smile as he strode forward.

"Shannon Erby, it *is* a pleasure." Ryder offered his hand, and Shannon placed hers into his.

"Likewise." Shannon warily eyed him as he lifted her hand and pressed his lips to her skin. She had to acknowledge he was even more gorgeous in the flesh, with his expertly styled sandy blond hair and mischievous gray eyes.

Shawn beamed as he cast a glance between the two of them. "Ryder, you're no stranger to television, I know, but I want you to trust Shannon's instincts when it comes to the show."

"Most definitely, I will." Ryder clapped the man on the shoulder. "This is going to be a great collaboration."

"I think so too." Shawn finished the contents of his flute. "Well, I'm going to let you two talk. Don't go far. Publicity shots will be happening very soon."

Shannon frowned. "You didn't tell me that was taking place tonight."

"Didn't I?" Shawn chuckled. "What are you worried about? You look picture perfect."

Shannon gritted her teeth as the executive producer walked off. She didn't appreciate his condescending tone or the way he kept springing things on her where the show was concerned.

"He's right, you know."

Shannon glanced at Ryder. "Excuse me?"

"You do look picture perfect." Ryder stopped a server and ordered a brandy. "You and I are going to look fantastic on screen together. I must admit, I'm quite a fan of yours. I think you have an amazing knack of making your guests feel at ease, no matter what is going on."

"Thanks, Ryder." Shannon finished her champagne and immediately wished she had a second glass. "I'm familiar with your work too."

"Familiar?" Ryder chuckled. "Does that mean you're not a fan?"

Shannon snagged another glass of bubbly from a passing server. "I admire your unwavering commitment not to hold anything back on television."

Ryder lifted an eyebrow. "Honesty is the best policy after all, right?"

"Yes, but I would imagine the delivery of your kernels of truth are hard for some to swallow sometimes." Shannon sipped her drink as Ryder chuckled.

"Hey, if you can't take the heat..."

"Get out of the kitchen." Shannon gave Ryder a bright smile. "I guess that notion will truly apply for our contestants."

"Yep." Ryder grinned. "We're going to have fun."

Shannon nodded even though she wasn't sure she agreed. "I'm looking forward to working with you."

"You know what?"

"What?"

Ryder leaned in toward her. "I don't believe you."

Shannon coughed as her champagne went down the wrong way. "E-excuse me?"

"You don't have to bullshit me, Shannon." Ryder paused as a server presented him with his brandy. "I'm sure you're less than thrilled to share the stage with a co-host. I would be, if I were you."

"Those are your words, not mine." Shannon had to work hard not to glare at Ryder when he laughed.

"My words, your feelings. I'd bet my life on that. Anyways, if we're going to work together, we need to be honest with one another. You see, I don't believe in kissing anyone's ass and I don't expect you to either." Ryder's gaze dipped briefly to her breasts. "Unless—"

"*Unless* you want the rest of my drink dripping from that thousand dollar haircut, I think you'd better stop while you're ahead." Shannon glared at Ryder when he roared with laughter.

"Easy, Erby." Ryder pointed his finger at her. "That's the fire we need to have everyone talking about with us as co-hosts. It's not just about the contestants on the show."

"We are here to help them shine."

"We're here to shine, period." Ryder lifted his hand and loosened his tie. "You're good at what you do. I respect that, but I will bring out a side of you that hasn't been seen yet, and I'm sure you'll do the same for me."

Shannon shook her head. "Well, it's confirmed. You are just as arrogant and boorish in person as you are on screen."

"And handsome. Don't forget handsome."

"Oh, please." Shannon downed the contents of her glass as Ryder chuckled.

"And you, Shannon, are not as sweet as I thought you were, thank God, but you are *every* bit as sexy in person."

Heat rose to Shannon's cheeks at the interest she saw in Ryder's assessing gaze. He was very attractive. She'd give him that. Attractive and aggravating as hell. A self-absorbed big mouth with dreamy gray eyes. Shannon understood exactly what Shawn had been thinking in adding Ryder to the cast as he joined them again.

"Well, how are my two new co-hosts getting along? Are our viewers going to be entertained?" Shawn cast a look between them and Shannon knew her face was turning as red as her hair.

"Absolutely." Ryder flashed another mega-watt smile. "I'm quite certain *Celeb Hotel Chef* will be one of the hot new shows of the season."

"Good, good." Shawn took hold of both of their arms. "Photo ops happening in twenty minutes by the sculpture. Ryder, Oliver Banner would like to meet you."

"Sure." Ryder winked at Shannon. "We'll get better acquainted later, Erby."

Shannon forced a smile when she wanted to roll her eyes as the two men strode off. Dear heavens, the man was incorrigible. Shannon had a feeling she was going to be put through her paces with him for the duration of the show's taping. She lifted her glass to her lips and sighed, discovering her drink was gone. Shannon took a step toward the bar and a wave of dizziness made her take pause. Deciding she needed food more than alcohol, Shannon started to make her over to the banquet table, stopping to speak to and greet people along the way. Conscious of photos constantly being taken, she kept a pleasant smile on her face and tried to ignore the dull throb beginning to beat behind her eyes.

Thirty minutes later, Shannon was completely out of sorts when she finally reached the lavish spread in front of her. She stared at the assortment of seafood, meat, cheeses and desserts, trying to decide what to eat that wouldn't make her sorry for her lack of discretion in the morning.

"I know the perfect bite for you."

Shannon turned her head in the direction of the deep voice carrying over the din in the room. Her pulse quickened when she met the warm gaze of Jay Dax, one of the chefs she and Aimee had recruited to compete on the show. "Hello, Jay."

Jay's smile was slow and sexy. "Hey. How are you, Shannon?"

"I'm well." Shannon felt a frisson of heat wind up her back as Jay nodded. She managed a grin as flashbacks of their unexpected kiss the last time she'd been in Vegas popped into her mind.

Jay's gaze dropped briefly to her lips. "Welcome back to Sin City."

"Thank you. How have you been?"

"Busy. Wondering how I let you and Aimee talk me into to juggling showbiz along with everything else I've got going on."

"We didn't have to twist your arm too much." Shannon snagged a cracker from the table. "Perhaps you've forgotten some of the details of that evening?"

The look Jay leveled at Shannon made her stomach flip-flop. "No. I haven't forgotten a single thing."

"Hmm." Shannon nibbled the cracker, silently cursing her poor choice of words. Pure Freudian. She'd wondered if he thought about the dinner they'd shared after Aimee had taken her leave. Shannon had been glad to enjoy a little more time alone with the charming, handsome chef.

Cocktails and conversation had flowed right up until Jay's attention had been needed in order to take care of some impending disaster in the five-star Banner hotel in which they'd dined. They'd both stood to say goodbye. Giggly and admittedly a little tipsy, Shannon had impulsively hugged him and had kissed him on the lips. A swirl of heat whooshed over her as she recalled the memory. To her credit, it had been a quick peck, but Jay had captured her face in his hands and kissed her again...a slow, sensual caress that still made her nipples harden when she thought about it. He'd walked away, leaving Shannon to stare after him. She'd chalked it all up to Jay's wicked drink menu and —

"Earth to Shannon?"

Shannon blinked and focused on Jay. "I'm sorry. What did you say?"

"I asked if you were hungry."

"Famished." Shannon cleared her dry throat, feeling parched from the salty cracker and her wayward thoughts. "You mentioned the perfect bite?

"I did. Want to taste it?"

Oh, my. Was he purposely trying to make her blush? Shannon kept her facial expression cordial and neutral, seeing nothing else in Jay's brown eyes but friendly anticipation. "Sure, Jay. Show me what you've got."

Jay winked at her. "With pleasure."

Shannon placed her hand on the table to steady herself as Jay grabbed a plate and went to work. She drew in a deep breath, disconcerted by another dizzy spell. First thing tomorrow she'd pick up some vitamin C. The last thing she needed was to come down with a cold right now. Shannon watched Jay place a slice of blue cheese on top of a piece of endive lettuce. Her stomached growled as he spooned some smoked crab dip on top, topped it with a tiny fig and sprinkled cracked pepper over it all.

"Taste." Jay offered her the small plate in his hand, and Shannon took hold of the beautifully displayed appetizer.

"Thanks, Jay." Shannon lifted the loaded endive leaf to her mouth and bit into it. Savory mixed with a hint of sweetness then burst into a myriad flavors and subtle heat. "Mmm…it's delicious."

"I'm glad you like it." Jay grinned. "Want more?"

Did she ever. Shannon nodded, struck again by Jay's presence and sex appeal. He was a dream for show business, attractive and charming, two things required for engaging television. "Yes, please. I'm so hungry."

"Mmm. My kinda woman, my favorite words." Jay winked at her as he went to task fulfilling her request.

Heaven help her, but what a smile. She'd forgotten how it made his warm brown eyes twinkle. The audience was going to eat him up. Shannon's gaze drifted down to the generous swell of Jay's lips as she remembered their spicy kiss. The man was one helluva kisser.

Jay set two more loaded endive leaves on her plate. "There you go."

"Thanks again, Jay." Shannon ate some more as Jay added a few strawberries next to her food.

"No problem." Jay popped a piece of fruit in his mouth. "I've always enjoyed watching beautiful women eat something I've prepared."

Shannon smiled while silently applauding herself for managing to finish another bite beneath Jay's steady gaze. "Too bad I'm not one of the judges. You'd definitely be at the top of my list."

"That's okay." Jay chuckled. "Just promise I'll be at top of your list, no matter what. I don't mind saying I wouldn't be here if you and Aimee hadn't convinced me to become a contender."

Shannon finished the bite of strawberry she'd taken. "Aimee was convinced you'd be a great fit for the show and once I met you, I agreed." She stepped closer to Jay when another member of the crew moved next to her for the crab dip.

"Well" — Jay tugged at his tie — "I can't wait to ditch this suit and get in the kitchen." He grabbed two more flutes from the server passing by and handed one to Shannon.

"Are you nervous?" Shannon took a sip of her drink, enjoying the way it complemented her food.

"I'm a little apprehensive." Jay gestured around the crowded space. "I like cooking for big events, not necessarily being one of the guests of honor. I've never needed to be in the spotlight. I know doing this show will change that, which has me questioning my decision to jump into what seems like the manic fray of reality television. That being said, I *am* ready to give this competition all I've got."

Shannon smiled. "I'm not going to lie and say your life isn't going to change. That's unavoidable once you step into the public eye."

"I know." Jay sipped his champagne. "I'm actually looking forward to having my work critiqued."

"You're going to do great." Shannon finished her champagne, grateful for the mellowing effect of the alcohol.

"How can you know that?"

"When you've been in the business as long as I have, you sometimes get a sense of these things." Shannon gave her plate to a server working behind the buffet table. "Besides my hunch, the fact—*facts*—remain that you're talented, personable and handsome. The camera is going to love you and you shouldn't be so hasty in ditching that suit. It looks damn good on you." Heat rushed to Shannon's face as Jay's grin widened. Clearly, she needed to curb her alcoholic intake around Jay. She didn't normally kiss a man first or dish out compliments to men when the cameras weren't rolling.

"Thank you, Shannon."

"You're welcome." Shannon cleared her throat, ignoring the prickles of awareness flitting over her. Her cheeks reddened again as she considered the fact he'd look damn good out of his suit too. "You now have my professional assessment, for whatever it's worth." Shannon lifted her glass to Jay with a bright smile. "Cheers."

She hoped he'd picked up her emphasis on the word 'professional'. Too bad the images in her mind of him stripping out of his clothing and kissing her again were anything but. She really needed to remedy her utterly lacking social life immediately.

When was the last time she'd had a date with a man she was truly interested in?

Chapter Two

Jay clinked his glass to Shannon's. "Cheers." He took another sip of champagne, tickled by the way she'd emphasized the word *professional*. There was no way she'd forgotten their kiss. "Coming from a gorgeous, talented woman like yourself...that assessment is worth a lot."

"I don't know about that." Shannon lifted a hand to smooth back her sleek tresses, drawing Jay's attention once more to the vibrant hue of her hair, so striking against her pale skin.

"I do." Jay was amused by her increasingly rosy cheeks. He speculated whether she was embarrassed by what he'd said or what she'd shared. She was adorable either way. No, Shannon was gorgeous. It was obvious she was aware of her beauty but she didn't come across as snobby or pretentious because of it. Jay had been surprised to discover how much he'd enjoyed talking with her over dinner.

"There you are, big brother."

Jay turned when he heard his sister's voice. "Hey." He gave Ari a quick hug. "I didn't think you were coming, after getting your text."

Ari waved her hand. "You *know* I wouldn't miss this." Ari shifted her gaze to Shannon.

Jay gestured toward Ari. "Shannon, this is my sister, Ari."

"I'm a big fan of yours, Ms. Erby." Ari pushed her long twists over her shoulder. "You are the sweetest, best-dressed host on television."

Shannon smiled. "I'm flattered. It's very nice to meet you. Do you live here?"

"I do. Moved here shortly after Jay did." Ari gave a dramatic sigh. "I've been trying to follow my dream of being on stage somewhere here ever since."

"Oh?" Shannon's green eyes widened with interest. "You're a singer?"

"Yes." Ari cast a glance at Jay. "I had an audition tonight. That's why I was late."

"And? How did it go?" Jay waited for Ari to answer, trying to read her face.

"And…" Ari squealed, jostling her glass of bubbly. "I got the job! It's a small lounge singer gig but it has potential to be more. The location is great. I'll be seen by many."

"Congratulations." Shannon tapped her flute against Ari's. "It's not easy getting your foot in the door. I haven't heard you sing but I can see why you were hired. The men will love looking at you while you perform. Women too. You're gorgeous."

"Thank you so much, Shannon." Ari beamed. "Coming from you, that means a lot." Ari frowned when they laughed. "What?"

"Your brother just said something similar a few minutes ago." Shannon touched Ari's arm. "I do hope this job blossoms into something more for you."

"I hope so too." Ari sighed. "I think things are finally going my way. It only took seven months for it to happen."

Shannon chuckled. "Hey, that's quick. One of these days, I'd love to hear you."

"I'll be performing every Tuesday and Thursday at the Peacock."

"Ooo, nice spot." Shannon shifted her gaze to Jay. "I'm guessing your sister is as gifted as you are?"

Jay grinned. "She's pretty damned talented."

"Then you'll do just fine, Ari. Better than fine." Shannon groaned as she waved to a member of the production crew. "Well, I'm being summoned." She glanced back at Jay. "Get ready to smile for the cameras. Thanks again for putting together those scrumptious bites."

"No problem, and I'll be ready." Jay watched Shannon walk off, wishing he'd had more time to talk to her. He'd planned on asking her out on an official date before she'd left Vegas weeks ago but hadn't gotten the opportunity. He'd been all right with that because the moment he'd seen her he'd planned to remedy the situation. Somehow, they were always interrupted before anything more could progress between them.

"Well, well, well…got your eyes on her, I see."

"Knock it off, Ari." Jay tore his gaze from Shannon's retreating form to glower at his gloating sister. "Practically the whole room does. I take that back. You've got several eyes on you, too." Jay pointed at her fuchsia cocktail dress. "Did I pay for that?"

"Uh huh. Like it?" Ari spun around, showing how the dress accentuated her curves.

"It's an attention grabber, just like you."

"Says the one about to become a TV sensation." Ari played with the gold bangles around her wrist. "So, you don't like it?"

"Ari, I love it but I'm sure I'm *not* going to like the bill." Jay frowned as Ari pouted. "I thought you agreed to no more frivolous spending."

"That was until I got a job. I have one." Ari smoothed a hand over her waist. "Besides, having a kick-ass dress to wear and wow everyone at this high-profile shindig *isn't* frivolous spending. First impressions are crucial."

"Just hand over your first check to me." Jay held back laughing when Ari's eyes widened.

"You aren't serious?" Ari groaned. "Look, I'll make you a deal, okay? My first priority is to get my own place. Doesn't that make you happy?"

Jay chuckled. "Very."

In truth, he'd been relieved when she'd told him she was moving to Las Vegas after he'd relocated. He'd made a promise to himself to always be in a position to help if she needed it after both their parents had died. The traveling distance between he and Ari had bothered him. He considered Ari to be one of his best friends and genuinely enjoyed having his little sister around. Still, he relished the thought of having his space all to himself again. "So, what did you sing?"

"*Lady Marmalade*." Ari rushed on to give him a note by note rundown of her audition, clearly thrilled to talk about anything other than money.

"I know you killed it."

Ari giggled. "You *know* I did." She pulled her chiming cell from her purse. "*Now*, he decides to call." His sister sighed. "I'll catch up with you?"

"Sure." Jay wondered who Ari was talking to as she walked away. He tried his damnedest to stay out of personal life, which wasn't always easy. Jay headed over to where the other cast members were gathering for the photo shoot. He was glad Ari had finally snagged a job she was excited about. Having her stay with him hadn't been a hardship, but Ari was fiercely independent and he knew she wanted to make her own way without him.

"Jay Dax, Sin City's chef extraordinaire."

Jay turned his head in the direction of his former classmate Oscar Blithe, one of the most talked about chefs in the biz. "Ah, we meet again, and here I thought I'd be up against some stiff competition."

Oscar shook his hand with a wry laugh. "Very funny, Jay. I see you haven't lost your bland sense of humor. I hope your cooking skills have improved because I do intend to win this thing."

"You do realize this is a five course competition?" Jay rubbed his chin, enjoying the challenging gleam in Oscar's eyes. "I seem to recall a certain cocky chef bombing more than once in our dessert courses."

"I have desserts mastered, Chef Dax." Oliver cleared his throat, shifting his gaze off Jay. "Speaking of dessert..."

"Good evening, gentleman. I'm Kelly Myer." Kelly moved between them, striking in her black dress and with teal-streaked blonde hair. "I'm thrilled to be up against such fierce competition."

"Hello, Kelly." Jay shook the petite woman's hand, surprised by her firm grip. "I'm Jay —"

"Dax." Kelly smiled. "I know." She turned her attention to Oscar. "And you would be?"

Jay chuckled, amused by the fierce glare Oscar shot him over Kelly's head.

"I'm Oscar Blithe. Executive chef for —"

"Well, well, well…I've been waiting to meet you three all day. I'm Denise Corliss." The pretty chef's smile was as sweet as caramel gelato as she shook everyone's hand in turn. "It's picture time." She pivoted and Jay's gaze drifted over her bared back in her sexy purple gown. Both women walked off, leaving Jay and Oscar to stare after them.

"Wow." Oscar shook his head as they followed the ladies. "I think these females are out for blood."

"Yeah." Jay caught sight of his sister, always the social butterfly, chatting with some people. He raised his chin when their gazes met and Ari lifted her glass.

"Is that your sister?"

Jay turned to see Oscar checking out Ari. "Yup."

"Introduce us after the photo shoot."

"Uh, uh." Jay chuckled. "I see you are still easily distracted by the fairer sex. Too bad I can't tell Kelly and Denise about their unknown advantage. Ah, well, I guess they'll figure it out soon enough, when you screw up due to your efforts to screw one of them."

Oscar scoffed. "This isn't culinary school. I can handle more than one dish at a time now, Jay."

Jay laughed as they joined the rest of the cast for *Celeb Hotel Chef* gathering in front of the photographer. Jay's gaze fell on Shannon and he wondered if he'd have to eat his own words about being distracted by a beautiful woman. Something about that redhead piqued his interest big time. It was more than just her looks, and after that kiss? Well, he wanted more — needed a chance to explore and savor more of

Shannon. There were layers to that woman that promised to be as delicious as his first taste of her.

Shannon cringed as the photographer whistled to grab everyone's attention. She stepped forward with Ryder beneath the bright lights in place for the photo shoot. A relative silence ensued and the excitement among the group was almost palpable. "Cast and crew of *Celeb Hotel Chef*, we will give our audience one hour of exciting, *delicious* television." Shannon acknowledged the cheers from the group by raising the gleaming trophy knife in her grasp.

"And if you guys don't make it one hour of exciting, delicious television"—Ryder leaned in toward Shannon—"Shannon and I will."

Shannon resisted the urge to jab Ryder with her elbow as good-natured laughs circled around them. "I'm sure I speak for Ryder as well as myself in saying we are rooting for you all." Shannon smiled at the chefs. "Oscar, Kelly, Denise and Jay, you are here because you are the best of the best. Having you four on *Celeb Hotel Chef* will set the bar high, and I for one can't wait for that first taste of excellence!"

"Yes!" Shawn Rill stepped up, clapping louder than everyone. "Thank you, Shannon and Ryder. If...no, *when* we hit that number one spot in the ratings, I will throw a bash of epic proportions." Shawn clapped the photographer standing to his left on the back. "Right. Now, let's take some pictures. David has a flight to catch in a couple of hours."

Shannon half-listened to David as he went about placing people to get the perfect shot. She moved forward when he asked for her, fixing a smile on her face as he positioned her in front of the contestants.

"Good. Now, Shannon, give me that sassy pose you usually do on the show." David stepped back with a nod. "Perfect. All right, don't move, folks, but give me brilliant smiles."

Shannon did as instructed, tuning out the low chatter behind her as David picked up his camera. Her feet ached in her stilettos and her tiny headache had morphed into a grumpy troll with a mallet in her head. She straightened her posture as everyone quieted and tried to add energy she didn't feel to her grin.

David worked fast, taking serious and playful pictures that Shannon couldn't wait to peek at. She breathed a sigh of relief when he finally declared he had what he needed. Shannon wondered how soon she could leave the party without appearing rude. Her tummy growled, making her wish she'd had more of the scrumptious bites Jay had put together for her.

"Well..." Ryder dragged a hand through his light locks. "I know I made you look damned good in those pictures."

Shannon chuckled. "Oh, please."

"You laugh, but when you see those pics, you'll declare they're the best damn snapshots ever." Ryder's gaze briefly shifted from Shannon to the blonde bombshell walking past them and he let out a low whistle. "I thought I'd greeted everyone at this party. If you'll excuse me?"

"Of course." Shannon smirked at Ryder. "Going to wow her with your mega-watt smile?"

"So, you noticed, huh?" Ryder grinned when she rolled her eyes. "Later, Erby."

Shannon shook her head as he sauntered off. Ryder was a wily combination of arrogance and charm. She couldn't decide if she liked or loathed him.

A prickle of awareness skittered down Shannon's spine. Someone was watching her, not an unusual occurrence, but she felt compelled to find out who it was. She turned her head and her eyes locked with Jay's. Her pulse reacted to the intensity of his gaze then he smiled, a friendly grin that made her question if she'd imagined the blatant male curiosity she'd seen. Her cell vibrated in her clutch, drawing her attention away from Jay. Shannon sighed when she saw it was Clarion, her mother, calling. She considered letting her voicemail pick it up then realized she'd rather get their conversation over now as opposed to later when she could finally relax. "Hello, Mum."

"Why did you wear a red dress to that premiere the other night? You know that's not your best color with your hair."

"Oh, Mother, really?" Shannon headed for the nearest exit, waving to a few people as she did. "You called me up to talk about my *clothes?*"

"Well, I thought we'd agreed on that deep purple number."

Shannon pushed the door open and stepped into the hallway, grateful to find it deserted, save one server rushing past her. "*You* suggested I wear it but my stylist selected the other dress because it looked better with the lighting for the set. I trust her judgment."

"Over your own mother?" Clarion made that disapproving noise in the back of her throat that Shannon detested. "Why am I not surprised?"

"Mum, while I appreciate your feedback, I pay Anna to make sure I look my best on screen. I trust her to do just that."

"Did Anna see the purple dress?"

"Yes." Shannon squeezed the bridge of her nose. She dropped her hand when a few people from the party came out into the hallway, laughing and with drinks in hand. "I will wear that dress. I promise."

"With your hair up."

"A great suggestion." Shannon leaned back against the wall, enjoying the coolness of it against her suddenly heated skin. "Is everything all right at home?"

"Everything's fine. What's that noise I hear?"

"I'm at the premiere party for *Celeb Hotel Chef*." Shannon smiled at the couple walking past her.

"Ah, yes. I'd forgotten that was tonight. How's it going?"

"Okay." Shannon knew her mother hadn't forgotten a thing. Clarion liked to keep tabs on everything she did. "I met my co-host."

"Who is it?"

"Ryder Stevens." Shannon considered slipping out of her stilettos as her mum clucked her approval. When she got back to her hotel room, she would make some tea in an attempt to ward off whatever bug was trying to take her down. "I was thrown for a loop when Shawn told me this morning. Do you know who he is?"

Clarion scoffed. "Of course. He's on that popular voice talent show. The two of you will look great on television together."

"Funny, Ryder went on about the same thing."

"He's right. He's also single, handsome and very rich."

Shannon blew out a breath. She knew where the conversation was headed now. "You can add pompous and attention-seeking to that list."

"Be nice and maybe he'll ask you out."

"I'm always nice, Mum. I know this may come as a shock but I'm not interested in Ryder."

"Why not? He's perfect for you. You two have so much in common." Clarion sighed wistfully. "Imagine the babies you'd make. You can't be intimidated by his persona and good looks."

"Oh, please. I'm not intimidated by Ryder in any way." Shannon shook her head. "Look, I've gotta go. Wanted for pictures." She hated lying but she needed to hang up before she screamed into the receiver. Besides, *someone* would want to snap her picture when she went back inside the bash.

"Okay. Wait...before you hang up, I wanted to let you know I'm thinking about coming to visit while you're taping the show."

Shannon's headache intensified at the thought of her mum hovering around in her world. "Really? That would require you to get on a plane. You know how much you hate flying."

"I know, but I really want to see Vegas, and what better time than now with you hosting and co-producing your own show out there? Honestly, I was surprised you didn't invite me to attend that party with you."

"I'm sorry." Shannon knew apologizing was easier than trying to explain why she'd rather not have her around. "We'll talk later?"

"Yes. Maybe you'll have good news about a date with Ryder by then."

"Goodbye, Mum. Love you." Her heart sank when Clarion hung up without a response. "Typical." Shannon sighed, wishing she had a closer relationship with her mum. Sometimes—most of the time—Shannon was convinced her mother only cared about her job, the status and glamour that went along with it. From pageants to proms, Clarion seemed to be only concerned about having the prettiest little girl.

Shannon pushed off the wall, determined not sink into a funk. She glanced at the clock on her phone and was surprised to see it was almost midnight. Shannon walked back to the entrance of the party, wanting nothing more than to just go back to her suite. She searched the crowd for Shawn with intentions of telling him she would leave soon. Shannon spotted the flashy producer in the center of the room, laughing with the female chef contenders, and she headed in his direction.

Shawn's face brightened when he saw her. "Shannon, I was looking for you. I need you on set by four tomorrow afternoon. There are some last minute changes I want to go over with you and Ryder."

"Last minute changes?" Shannon kept her voice light when she wanted to bark at the hyperactive producer.

Shawn waved his hand. "Nothing you can't handle."

"Oh, I'm sure of that." Shannon gave him and the female chefs a tight smile, annoyed by Shawn's slightly patronizing tone. "Can I steal you away for a minute, Shawn?"

"Of course." Shawn stepped to her. "Everything okay? You don't look like your usual bubbly self."

"You know, I'm not feeling the best. I'm actually getting ready to head back up to my room so I can be fresh for tomorrow's taping."

Shawn nodded his head. "Yes. I need you to give me the level of energy our viewers have come to expect." Shawn frowned as he studied her. "You're not coming down with the flu or something are you?"

"I don't think so." Shannon forced a grin. "I think I just need a good night's rest."

"All right." Shawn glanced at his watch. "I'll see you later then."

"Yes, you will. Good night."

"Night, Shannon. Feel better."

"Thanks, Shawn." Shannon offered a small smile to him as he pivoted before doing the same. After saying goodbye to various people, she headed for the exit once again. She exhaled with relief when she finally pushed through the doors then gasped when she walked right into Jay.

"Whoa." Jay reached out to touch her arm. "I'm sorry."

Shannon lifted her hand. "No, that was my fault." She gazed up at Jay and was instantly drawn to the warmth shimmering in his brown eyes.

"Leaving?"

"I am." Shannon shivered when he released his hold on her, surprised by a wave of dizziness that made her sway toward him. What was wrong with her today?

"Hey, are you okay?"

The concern in Jay's voice touched Shannon. "Y-yes. Just tired and hungry."

"Hungry?" Jay frowned. "I left you *hungry?* That's unacceptable."

Shannon waved her hand. "Not your fault again. I'm going to go up to my room, fix a quick bite then crash."

"Do you have a kitchenette in your suite?"

"Yes." Shannon offered Jay a wobbly smile. "Yes, I do. A nice feature, given my extended stay here. Now ask me if I'll cook in it."

"Will you cook in it?"

"Probably not most nights. I'm usually too tired, like now. I like cooking but my self-prepared meals tend to consist of soups, salads and sandwiches."

"That's still better than constantly eating out—unless you're eating at my restaurant." Jay smiled when Shannon chuckled. "Why don't you let me whip something up for you?"

Shannon's pulse leaped at Jay's proposal. A swirl of heat whorled within her as memories of the last time they'd shared a meal skated through her mind. "Oh, Jay. I can't ask you to do that."

Jay grinned. "You *didn't* ask me. I offered. Look, you're clearly exhausted and it would be my pleasure to cook for you."

"Hmm…"

"I promise whatever I make will be tastier than any soup, salad or sandwich you fix."

"Oh, I'm sure." Shannon warmed beneath Jay's steady, expectant gaze. All of her reservations began to melt away as considered how nice it would be to take Jay up on his offer. She *was* exhausted, and having a seasoned chef prepare a quick meal was exactly what she wanted—needed—at the moment.

"Well, what do you say, Shannon?"

Shannon exhaled then nodded. "Yes."

Chapter Three

Jay tossed the avocado and tomato salad he'd prepared with freshly squeezed lime juice and sea salt while half-listening to Shannon talk to someone on the phone. He loved her voice, found her accent—like the rest of her—sexy as hell. Offering to prepare food for her had been an impulsive, risky move but it had paid off. He was finally getting some time alone with her, even if it was only on a professional level.

Jay glanced at Shannon, observing her stiff posture and cool tone. It was obvious that whomever she was speaking to was getting on her nerves. His own cell vibrated on the countertop and he glanced at it to see an incoming text from his sister. He unlocked his phone to read her message.

Real party started after you left!

With a barely muted groan, Jay sat his cell down. He could only guess what kind of mischief Ari had gotten into—knowing her, it probably involved a man. She seemed to be a magnet for knuckleheads. Worse yet, she was attracted to playboys. Jay exhaled as he took his sizzling omelet out of the skillet. At least she wasn't gambling. They were going to have a conversation she didn't like if he had to lend her more money.

"Sorry 'bout that." Shannon placed her phone on bar counter and faced the mini kitchenette. "Shawn would've had a conniption if he called back for some reason and couldn't reach me so close to taping. I'm half tempted to shut that damn thing off for the rest of the night."

"You and me both." Jay slid half of the omelet he'd fixed onto the plate in front of her. "I swear my sister sends me a million texts a day."

"Ari has an effervescent personality." Shannon placed a cloth napkin on her lap.

"That she does. There's never a dull moment when she's around…a quiet one either, for that matter."

Shannon grinned. "I'm an only child, so I can't relate. You two are close then?"

"We are." Jay sat a bowl with the avocado salad next to Shannon's plate. "Ari actually lives with me at the present moment."

"Aww….how nice"—Shannon gestured to her food—"she gets to eat like this all the time. Jay, this is wonderful. Wow, you really did whip up something delicious using only a few grocery items."

Jay smiled. "Nothing to it. You had some essentials and an impressive spinning wheel of spices."

"Ha! I saw that at the market and couldn't resist buying it—you know, for those meals I *don't* usually cook."

Jay chuckled. "You bought them because you enjoy cooking."

"I do." Shannon picked up her fork then waved it. "I'm no chef but I can make eggs." She took a bite of the omelet then moaned appreciatively. "Wait, not like this, though. What did you put in this?"

"Cheddar cheese, mushrooms, a little tarragon and dill." Jay rinsed off a few strawberries then placed them on Shannon's plate.

"Delicious." Shannon ate some more with little sighs of delight that tickled Jay.

"Thank you."

Shannon lifted her face to his. "No, thank you, Jay. What a noble thing you've done in my little kitchen."

"It's my pleasure, as I said before." Jay watched her taste the salad, noticing the blooming color in her cheeks. "Like it?"

"Love it." Shannon glanced around him at the kitchenette. "I don't know how you did all this so fast without having a messy space to show for your efforts."

"I still have a pan and spatula to clean." Jay moved to the sink, cursing his less-than-noble thoughts. Shannon hadn't given him any indication she was interested in him for anything other than his culinary skills. Jay considered the possibility that the kiss they'd shared had been a spur of the moment kind of thing, no real attraction involved on Shannon's part.

"You don't have to wash those, Jay. Seriously. You've done enough."

Jay glanced at her over his shoulder as shook his head. "No way. You eat. I never leave a kitchen in which I've cooked in a disarray." He winked at her before turning to the sink. "Goes against a culinary code instilled within me a while back." Jay turned on the faucet, smiling as Shannon giggled.

"Oh? Did you learn this code in school?"

"Nope." Jay washed up the few dishes remaining then turned off the water. He reached for a towel then pivoted to face Shannon as he dried his hands. "My mom. She could cook huge meals and somehow keep everything neat and tidy in the kitchen. I learned so many things from her. Would you like any salt or pepper?"

"No need. You've seasoned everything perfectly." Shannon reached for her napkin when it started to slip off her lap. "I haven't had time to eat a decent meal all day. I know I would've just grabbed a yogurt then crashed if I'd come up alone."

"I'm glad you didn't." Jay placed the dry towel on the counter. A wayward strand slipped free of Shannon's bun, drawing Jay's attention, and he contemplated how good it would feel to have those ginger tresses intertwined around his fingers again as he angled her beautiful face for a second kiss. Blood pumped faster through Jay's veins as he met Shannon's steady gaze.

Damn it all to hell, but it was time to go. "All right, Shannon. Can I get you anything else?"

"No, thank you." Shannon lifted another forkful of the omelet. "I'm going to try adding those spices the next time I attempt to make one of these."

"Do you have trouble flipping the egg?"

Shannon groaned. "Every single time. Got any tips for that?"

"I'd have to show you. Trust me, making the perfect omelet is an easily learned technique."

"You haven't seen my omelets." Shannon wrinkled her nose as she took another bite and Jay chuckled. "I might hold you to that cooking lesson, Chef Dax."

"Okay." Jay smiled as he picked his phone up. He slipped the slim device into his pants pocket, regretfully ready to make his exit. "Well, my job here is done." He reached for his suit jacket, laying across the bar stool next to him, thinking he deserved a gold star for his absolute professionalism in the face of his growing attraction to Shannon. "I'm going to go and let you finish your meal in peace."

"Wait, you're not going to eat with me?" Shannon frowned, surprised and disappointed Jay didn't want to stay. She couldn't remember the last time she'd invited a man up to her room who'd left before trying to sleep with her. Maybe that kiss they'd shared hadn't been as amazing as she'd thought. Jay's cordial conduct after their unexpected lip-lock had impressed her as much as his mastery in the kitchen. "I can't eat that whole omelet, scrumptious as it is."

"I wanted you to have some for in the morning." Jay flashed another one of his sexy grins her way.

"Oh, how thoughtful." Shannon took another bite, watching him as he unrolled and buttoned his sleeves then proceeded to put on his suit jacket. She couldn't help but notice the unmistakable outline of his biceps as he did.

Dear heavens, the man is gorgeous. Tall, good looking, kind and a beast in the kitchen? There was no *way* he was single. Shannon looked down at her food with the realization she was curious about his personal life—curious about him period.

"Now what are you sighing about?"

Shannon lifted her head up to meet Jay's amused gaze, unaware of audibly exhaling.

"Concerned about the calories? I assure you that meal will only set you back about six hundred."

"No, it isn't that." Shannon sat down her fork. "I've never paid much attention to calories."

"No?"

"Uh uh." Shannon gave him a bright smile, confused by the spark of interest she knew she'd sensed from Jay earlier. She'd tried to push their little erotic episode from her mind but then he'd proposed making her dinner. Naturally, she'd wondered if he too had been curious about exploring the unspoken chemistry between them. He'd done a fantastic job, was clearly ready to go and now she didn't want him to.

"Sorry. I assumed with your figure you counted every single one."

"I've always been naturally thin. Hated it when I was in school. I was tall and awkward and my classmates called me Beanpole Red."

Jay chuckled. "Ouch."

"Yes." Shannon lifted a hand to smooth her hair, a little embarrassed by her omission. "Thankfully, I grew into my body."

Jay's gaze flicked over her. "Yes, you certainly did."

A beat of silence ensued and Shannon's pulse accelerated as Jay studied her.

"So, why that sigh, Red?"

Shannon smiled, charmed by the nicer nickname and the curiosity layered within the deep tones of Jay's deep voice. "I guess, I just figured you'd share the meal you prepared with me."

"And I didn't want to presume you had invited me up to your room for anything other than my professional services."

"Okay, I'm inviting you to join me for dinner." Shannon lifted her chin, determined not to show her discomfiture beneath Jay's amused gaze. "Would you join me, Jay? I get tired of eating alone."

"I'd love to." Jay smiled at her before going back into the kitchen.

Shannon let out a breath she didn't realize she was holding as she listened to him grab a plate. "Great."

"You know what we're missing?"

"What?" Shannon picked up her fork and took another bite of savory egg as Jay joined her at the bar counter with the other half of her omelet.

"Something to drink." Jay shrugged out of his suit jacket again and placed it on the back of his chair. "I saw a white wine in the fridge—and orange juice. Which would you prefer?"

Shannon leaned back in her seat, crossed her legs, assessing the butterflies in her stomach. "Would white wine compliment this meal?"

"White wine will pair nicely." Jay went back into her temporary kitchen, finding her wine glasses before she could open her mouth to tell them where they were. He returned a moment later with two goblets and the wine in tow. "I love this winery. I had the privilege of touring and tasting the company's upcoming blends last summer."

"Really?" Shannon moved her legs as he took his seat next to hers. She watched him open the bottle and pour, accepting her glass with a smile. "Thank you."

"You're welcome." Jay poured wine in his glass then lifted it. "Let's toast."

"Okay." Shannon lifted her goblet. "To…?"

"Unexpected challenges."

Shannon raised an eyebrow. "Unexpected challenges?"

"Yes. I'm sure you've already encountered some working for *Celeb Hotel Chef,* and I'm sure I'm about to experience a few of my own as a contestant on the show."

"Ahh." Shannon clinked her glass to his with a laugh. "I can definitely drink to that." She blew out a breath after they both took a sip. "Ryder is a bit of an ass. Oops. Did I just say that?"

Jay chuckled as he sat down. "Yep, you did. I wish I could say I hadn't noticed. He clearly thrives on being in the spotlight, but then again, so do you."

"I'm *accustomed* to being in the spotlight. That doesn't mean that I *thrive* beneath it." Shannon shrugged. "Showbiz is just the path I wound up on, much to my mother's joy and encouragement."

"So, what are you saying?" Jay sat down and placed a napkin on his lap. "You don't enjoy being on television?"

"I don't hate it. It's what I do. I'm good at it but sometimes I wonder what my life would be like if I'd taken another path...a less invasive one. My social life—or lack thereof—is constantly under the microscope. I always have to look my best, smile wide and pretend that my life isn't anything other than fabulous." Shannon pushed her plate away. "I'm a real person. I have bad days, bad hair days but in TV-land...that's not allowed." Shannon shifted her gaze from Jay, who'd stopped eating to look at her. "I'm sorry. You must think I'm a whiny brat."

Jay finished his bite while shaking his head. "No. I don't think that at all. You're under a lot of pressure and somehow you manage to handle it all with an extreme amount of grace. Do you ever take time out for yourself?"

Shannon scoffed. "Hardly. My insane schedule doesn't usually allow it."

"Then it isn't your schedule, Red. This is your life." Jay sliced into the corner of his omelet. "You've got to find a way to get the balance you need to be truly happy."

Unexpected tears filled Shannon's eyes as she lifted her face to Jay's. "Is there such a thing, Jay? True happiness?"

Jay shrugged. "True as in pure happiness? I don't know. I think we have to constantly strive to be happy with ourselves, others and all the craziness life can throw at you. Professional and personal contentment is a goal of mine."

"Me too." Shannon lifted her glass and finished its contents.

"Would you like a refill?"

"Please." Shannon drew in a shaky breath as Jay got up and brought the bottle over. She watched him pour more wine into her glass and decided to throw caution to the wind as he sat back down. "Are you single, Jay?"

Jay sat the bottle on the counter and looked at her, amusement twinkling in his warm brown eyes. "I am. Why do you ask?"

"I-I just wanted to know." Shannon took another generous sip of her drink, aware of his gaze upon her.

"Why, Shannon?"

Shannon set her wine glass down then turned in her chair to face Jay. "Because I haven't been able to erase our kiss from my mind." Spirals of heat unfurled within her as she continued and she momentarily broke eye contact with Jay. "I know this might sound crazy...but there's just something about you. I've imagined you kissing me again...and I've wondered if you've done the same thing."

The beats of silence that ensued wreaked havoc on Shannon's equilibrium. Her gaze fell briefly to Jay's mouth when he started to smile.

"Have I thought about our unexpected kiss? Hell yes, and I'm glad you brought up the subject. I've absolutely envisioned kissing you again."

Shannon's pulse reacted to the sensual curve of Jay's lips quicker than to the alcohol in her glass. "You have?"

"Of course."

His admission warmed her blood, made her lean in his direction. "Mmm. Well, what are you waiting for then?"

Jay grinned, a slow predatory slant of his lips that sent a shiver across Shannon's spine. "Just one kiss?"

"One kiss."

Jay nodded. "All right."

Tingles of awareness and anticipation scattered goosebumps over Shannon's skin as he shifted in his chair to face her, enclosing her legs with his own.

"One kiss, Red."

Shannon closed her eyes, anticipating his mouth on hers. His kiss made her hot and wet as he moved his lips across hers. She moaned in her throat beneath his sensuous onslaught, parting her lips, welcoming the taste of him. She wanted more as Jay pushed his fingers in her hair. Shannon didn't think she'd ever been kissed so thoroughly, so reverently. Her heartbeat thundered in her ears when he pulled back, his cheek still pressed against hers.

"Woman, you taste even better than I remember." Jay brushed his lips against her earlobe.

"Likewise." Shannon lifted her face to kiss him again, and Jay obliged her. She slipped her hand up over his back, savoring the feel of hard muscles beneath her fingertips as he deepened their kiss, taking complete control. Shannon groaned with need as he gripped her hair tighter, loving the slight twinge of discomfort mingled with the pleasure of his mouth on hers. She was breathless when Jay pulled back, unable to do anything more than stare into his eyes.

"That was more than one kiss." Jay's voice was gruff, the only evidence he was as affected by her as she was him.

"I know. One wasn't enough." Shannon reached up to touch Jay's dreads, wondering what it would feel like to have his thick hair brush across her sensitive nipples.

"Satisfied now?"

Shannon giggled. "Are you?"

"I asked you first." Jay slowly brought strands of her hair up to his nose and breathed in deeply. "Damn, you smell good."

"Thank you." Shannon moved her hands off his back and placed them on his muscular thighs. "We're both avoiding your question."

"Look, I'm not going to pretend that I don't want to pick you up, take you to bed and ravish every inch of you. I do. I'm rock hard at the promise of how delicious that would be."

Shannon barely suppressed a shiver of longing. "Oh, my…" Her panties were damp from all the erotic possibilities that could unfold between them. "Yes."

"Mmm hmm. Yes." Jay moved back from her. "But this isn't the right moment for us."

Shannon frowned. "What?"

"You've had an exhausting day." Jay stood, towering over her. "You have to get up early."

"Oh. Okay." Shannon rose to her feet, shocked by Jay's flat-out refusal to take her to bed. When had that ever happened? She walked with him to the door, trying to figure out what to say next.

Jay placed one hand on the door handle then turned to her and chuckled. "Don't look like that, Red."

"Like what?" Shannon straightened her back and gave him her television smile. She was annoyed with herself that he'd caught sight of her unguarded facial expression.

"Like you're disappointed and confused." Jay wrapped his arm around her then brought her body close to his. Accustomed to being taller than most men, Shannon realized that even in her heels she came only up to Jay's chin. Her eyes widened when he pressed her against his hard-on. "Make no mistake. I want you and when we *do* go further than a few kisses, I don't want to have to worry about depleting your already-taxed reserves." Jay kissed her hard then released her. "Trust me. You're going to need all your strength. Good night, Shannon."

His words and the dark desire glimmering in his eyes made Shannon nipples harden. Rendered momentarily speechless, she cleared her throat as Jay opened the door. "Jay?"

He pivoted to look at her. "Yes?"

"Do you offer cooking lessons professionally?"

"No. That offer is just for you. Anytime, anywhere." Jay stepped out into the hallway.

"But not tonight?" She couldn't resist testing his resolve, still couldn't believe he was walking away from her open invitation to stay. Shannon grinned as Jay laughed. She loved the deep sound of it bouncing off the walls.

"Get some rest. We'll cook later."

Shannon watched him walk off, smiling wide. There was no mistaking the sexy promise in his tone. Shannon closed her door, barely stifling a yawn. Jay was right. She was exhausted...and aroused as hell.

Shannon kicked off her heels and padded over to the dishes on the bar counter. She took another bite of Jay's salad and let out a little moan of delight.

The man was as delicious as his food. Shannon reached up to tweak her hard nipple through her dress. She needed to come. Shannon parted her lips to curse Jay for leaving her in such a state then closed her mouth. She respected and admired him for calling it a night. He'd succeeded in making her want him even more. Shannon absently caressed her breast, thinking about Jay. His lips…his kiss. She had no doubt they'd cook later. They would sizzle.

Chapter Four

Jay eyed the other chefs standing at their stations and wondered if they were as confident as he was about making it to the next round in the five course cook-off competition. He tried and failed to catch a glimpse of Ari in the sea of distorted faces beneath the lights. She'd promised to be cheering him on but he hadn't seen her before moving to his station. Jay glanced around the set, amazed by the fully functional mini kitchens that had been designed for each chef. Thunderous applause erupted from the audience as Shannon made her way onto the stage, a vision of beauty in a striking purple dress.

"Welcome to the premiere of *Celeb Hotel Chef*. I'm your host, Shannon Erby."

"And..." Ryder's voice could be heard off in the distance. A spotlight landed on him and the audience went nuts again. "I'm your host, Ryder Stevens." Ryder walked up and stood beside Shannon, a wide grin on his face. "Wow. Doesn't she look amazing?" Ryder's question to the audience garnered even more applause and a few cat calls.

"Thank you, Ryder."

Shannon's smile was brilliant. She'd pulled her hair away from her face in a low, sleek side ponytail and the wavy ginger strands brushed against her cleavage. Jay wished he'd had a moment to tell her before the show began how gorgeous she looked but there had been no time. No matter, there would be later. He'd make sure of it.

"You look dapper yourself, Ryder." Shannon acknowledged her co-host and the appreciative crowd. "It's going to be fun hosting this tasty show with you."

"I've gotta say, standing up here with you is certainly going to be delicious." Ryder briefly lifted his mic as the audience cheered. "Let's meet the chefs, shall we?"

"Absolutely." Shannon stepped over to Oscar. "Oscar Blithe, executive chef for Terra Resort, located in California, are you ready to cook?"

"Oh, I'm ready to *burn*, Shannon." Oscar laughed as the crowd twittered. "Not my food" — he pointed at Jay, Kelly and Denise — "my competition."

Shannon chuckled as the audience clapped. "Your competition are all at the top of their game. Who do you see as your biggest threat?"

Oscar folded his arms as he shook his head. "*I* am the threat, Shannon. I came to win and that's what I'm going to do."

"Well, Ryder, Oscar's said more than a mouthful." Shannon moved over to Jay as Ryder agreed.

"That he has. I don't think he realizes the talent he's up against, does he, Kelly?"

"No, but that's okay." Kelly glared at Oscar before smiling triumphantly at Ryder. "He'll learn." She waved a spatula at the cheering people.

Ryder nodded. "Coming to us from the Mandarin Ori in New York, Kelly Myer has enjoyed sweet success as their executive chef. Is it safe to say you'd like to see Oscar go home first?"

"Hmm." Kelly wrinkled her nose. "I wouldn't dare answer that question, but let's just say I've learned that certain foods, like people, have a very short shelf-life."

Jay chuckled along with everyone else as Ryder moved over to Denise and Shannon lifted her mic to him.

"Jay Dax, you're executive chef for the Banner Hotel right here in Las Vegas." Shannon paused for the applause before looking back at Jay. "Has working in Sin City equipped you for this contest?"

"Absolutely." Jay grinned, noticing color blooming in Shannon's cheeks as she talked. "Enjoying great food is one of life's pleasures and I've been told many times my dishes deliver."

Shannon glanced at the enthusiastic audience. "I think we'd all like to hear more."

"My food speaks for itself." Jay shrugged, directing his attention to the seated people. "Besides, we all know what happens in Vegas…"

Shannon giggled as the audience finished the line. "Ryder, do you believe enjoying great food is one of life's pleasures?" She moved away from Jay to stand by a curtain hiding the panel of judges and he admired her gold stilettos and long legs…legs he wanted wrapped around him as soon as possible.

"Indeed." Ryder turned to Denise. "Denise Corliss is one of the executive chefs for The Peninsula Chicago. Tell me, Chef Corliss, do you agree with Jay's statement?"

"I do. Sharing a scrumptious meal with family, friends or a lover can be a magical experience and" — Denise eyed Jay — "*I've* been told I can make magic happen in the kitchen."

"Well, Chef Corliss, you're going to get the chance here very shortly to make magic happen." Ryder joined

Shannon. "We've kept the judges a secret up to now. What do you say, Shannon? Should we reveal our celebrity judges?"

The audience went wild as Shannon nodded. "Let's do it."

Jay clapped along with the hosts as the curtain was slowly pulled to reveal the three judges. He was excited to recognize them all.

"I'm thrilled to have Misha Banner, our *Celeb Chef* winner last year as one of our esteemed judges." Shannon beamed as Misha waved to the crowd.

"She is joined by Bernard Dobi, a renowned food critic and author of the book *Culinary Dos and Don'ts.*" Ryder waited until the applause abated somewhat before continuing. "And last, but certainly not least, Don Mackey. His desserts have been served at the White House and enjoyed around the country. Don, you'll have to wait for the sweet stuff. Tonight's competition is focused on the first course. Our chefs will be preparing soups and salads."

"That's not a problem." Don chuckled. "I can't wait to sample whatever these fine chefs present to us."

"Shannon, what's tonight's secret ingredient?" Ryder's grin widened as the enthusiastic twittering in the audience increased.

Jay watched Shannon open an envelope, admiring the way her red locks shimmered beneath the lights. His cock twitched as he recalled how silky her hair had felt between his fingers as he'd kissed her, making him almost regret leaving her room when he could've stayed. Shannon had wanted him to and he'd almost changed his mind when she'd tried to tempt him. God, she was sexy — so poised and sweet.

"The secret ingredient is…" Shannon paused for dramatic flair. "Brussel sprouts!"

Jay grinned when he heard Kelly groan behind him. He wasn't worried. He knew just what he planned to do with that vegetable — and with Shannon.

* * * *

"I decided the ponytail was better. That's why." Shannon sighed, wishing guilt hadn't prevented her from letting her mum's call go to voicemail.

"I guess it worked. I still think pulling your hair *all* the way up would've shown off that gorgeous neckline even more." Clarion clucked her tongue. "I bet you they'll be talking about your dress on that entertainment show in the morning."

Shannon uttered some sound, trying not to come across as indifferent. "So how's the weather in Cali?"

"A little chilly for this time of year. I swear it's getting colder here. Makes me think I never should've left home to be with you here."

Shannon chuckled. "Come on. You get way more warm, sunny days being in California than in the UK."

"I'm glad you're reminding me of that right now." Clarion sighed. "Let's talk about something less mundane than the weather."

"Okay." Shannon smoothed moisturizer on her face.

"I've got a surprise for you."

"Oh?" Shannon glanced at the clock on the wall. She had less than five minutes before Jay arrived and she still hadn't decided on what to wear. She tossed two sundresses aside before selecting a black and white sheath dress. Shannon placed her cell on the bed, hit speakerphone then cursed when it slid on the floor. She rushed to retrieve and put it up to her ear.

"What was that noise?"

"Sorry, Mum, the phone fell." Shannon stepped into the dress and pulled it up over her purple lingerie.

"What are you doing?"

Shannon pivoted in the mirror, finally pleased with her attire. She didn't want to be dressed too sexily for her cooking lesson. "I'm going to dinner."

"On a date?"

"No." It wasn't a lie. Technically, she and Jay hadn't called it anything other than a lesson in the culinary art of making flawless omelets. Shannon couldn't wait to see if Jay stuck to his strictly professional code as her teacher tonight.

"That's too bad. You have great chemistry with Ryder. Tabloids say he's single. He hasn't asked you out? I can tell he likes you."

"No, Mother, and I hate to break it to you, but what you're seeing is just great television. Ryder likes Ryder."

Clarion sighed. "I wanted you to have a career in showbiz but I also wanted some grandkids while I could still move around."

Frustrated, Shannon rolled her eyes at her mother's familiar litany. "Oh, geez. You're moving faster than half the women in your subdivision. Must you give me this guilt trip every few months? I'm sorry I don't have it all for you. I'm trying to juggle work and jumpstarting my flailing personal life the best I can, okay?" Shannon flopped on the bed, wishing she'd bitten her tongue instead of speaking her mind when Clarion remained silent. "Mum…I'm sorry. I didn't mean to yell."

"Well, you did." Clarion huffed, clearly unable to see a reason for apologizing herself.

Shannon rubbed the bridge of her nose, mentally exhausted. She rose from the bed at the sound of knocking. "I have to go."

"All right. We'll talk later."

Shannon stared at her phone as the line went dead, dismayed by how the call had gone. "Damn." She wished she hadn't let her mother push her buttons. More incessant knocking had her racing to the door. She opened it and instantly felt better when she saw Jay. "Hello."

"Good evening."

The slow curve of Jay's lips made Shannon's heart race. Without her heels on, she had to lift her chin to meet his eyes. "Congratulations on completing the first round, Chef Dax. I sampled your appetizer. Brussel sprouts never tasted so good." Shannon stepped aside to let him in, her gaze drawn to his physique—expertly accentuated in the dark jeans and white shirt he wore. He moved past her, blessing Shannon with the subtle and yet intoxicating scent of his cologne.

"Why, thank you." Jay's electric smile seemed to zing her right down to her toes.

"You're welcome." Shannon released her hold on the door for it to close. "Although, I do feel bad for Denise. I didn't expect the judges to cut her first because of her soup."

"I know. Soups can be tricky. She was in good spirits when she left though." Jay smiled at her as he lifted a small grocery bag. "Are you ready to cook?"

"I am." Shannon turned back to the door when it didn't click shut and pushed until it did. "What's in the bag? I stocked up for my lesson." She pivoted to face him then frowned when she saw him studying her with rapt attention. "What is it?"

Jay sat the bag in his arm down on the table then walked over to her. "Your dress. It's not zipped in the back."

Shannon's eyes widened as she glanced over her shoulder to confirm Jay's observation. "Oops." Flustered by her mum, she'd forgotten about the zipper. "I was distracted."

Jay shook his head. "Now, so am I."

Shannon smiled as she turned her back to him. "Zip me up?" She shivered when Jay slipped his hands inside her dress to caress her shoulders.

"I don't think I can." Jay moved her hair out of the dress then pressed his lips against her neck and Shannon's pulse leaped. "In fact, I know I can't."

Shannon leaned against him, loving his hands on her skin. Her body warmed all over as he continued to caress her. Tamped down desire ignited and spread like wildfire within her.

"All I've thought about is touching you, kissing you." Jay turned her to face him. "I can't get the taste of your lips out of my head."

"Mmm. I suffer from the same problem where you are concerned." Shannon stared up into his handsome face, a little in awe at the raw need she saw in Jay's eyes. "I want you to taste more." She reached up, pushed the parted dress from her shoulders and let it fall in a pool around her bare feet.

"So gorgeous." Jay traced the purple lace flower on her bra and Shannon's nipples puckered.

She unhooked her bra and tossed it onto the chair nearby. Her breath hitched in her throat when Jay simply stared at her breasts.

"Fuck. So fucking perfect."

"Touch me, Jay." Shannon trembled when he obliged, cupping her breasts in his large hands. She looked down as he toyed with her nipples, getting wetter by the second from his ministrations and the erotic contrast of their skin. Breathless, Shannon tugged at Jay's shirt. "I want to touch too."

Jay grinned as he released his hold on her. He stripped out of his T-shirt, and Shannon reached out to squeeze his hard biceps. "Yum."

Jay flexed for her. "Like that?"

"Love that. I'd think you were a fitness instructor over a chef if I didn't know."

"Not all chefs are overweight." Jay winked at her as he extracted a condom from his pocket.

Shannon took it from him. "No. Some are sexy as hell." She grinned as he unbuttoned and unzipped his pants, pushed them down and stepped out of them. Her gaze drifted over his tight abs to the impressive tent in his underwear. She wet her bottom lip as he yanked his boxers down and stepped out of them, revealing his thick cock.

"Touch me, Red."

Shannon wrapped her hand around his erection as she lifted her face to his. She moaned as he claimed her lips in a hungry kiss, aware that she'd soaked her panties. He was so hard and big and she wanted every inch of him inside her. She gently squeezed his cock when he broke the kiss, smiling at his gruff groan. "Are we going to have sex in the kitchen?"

"Not this time."

Shannon let go of him as he scooped her up and carried her to the bedroom. She giggled when he placed her on top of the comforter, tossing the foil packet within her grasp in his direction. Shannon lifted her bottom to help him remove her sodden panties, feeling heated from head to toe. "Red everywhere." Shannon watched Jay beneath hooded eyes as his gaze drifted between her legs to her bare pussy, save the trimmed triangle on top.

"I see. Delicious." Jay stroked his cock with one hand. "I want to see more."

"Do you?" She knew her entire body had to be flushed with her rising need to be taken.

"Yes."

Shannon parted her thighs and the cool air on her heated, slick flesh scattered goosebumps over her skin. She wasn't accustomed to her lovers taking their time once clothes were off. Luckily, she knew how to make herself come and usually did during sex.

"Play with your pussy for me. Spread those juices all over so I can fully appreciate your taste when I put my mouth on you."

Somehow Shannon managed to blush harder as she slipped her hand between her legs. She dipped her fingers into her wetness, teased her engorged clit and moaned.

"Finger-fuck yourself." Jay's voice had deepened.

Shannon's breath hitched as she obeyed. "Jay, please." Her eyes dipped to his bobbing erection and she tightened her sheath around her fingers in anticipation of being filled — no, stuffed — with Jay's cock.

"Don't worry. I know what you need." Jay got on his knees and lowered his head between her quivering thighs. "Mmm. You're so wet for me. I love that."

Shannon gasped at the exquisite sensations flooding through her from warmth of his mouth on her sensitive flesh. She arched her back as he began to flick her clit with slow, languid strokes of his tongue. Shannon pushed her damp fingers in his hair and grabbed hold of a few dreads when pushed his tongue inside her. "Oh, God…" She didn't recognize the sound of her own voice as she ground her pussy on Jay's face, needing to reach the sweet pinnacle that was so close it was within her reach.

Shannon brought her hands up to her breasts when Jay went back to concentrating on her clit, sucking and licking her. She teased her nipples, mewling with delight and surprise when he slid two fingers inside her. Her gasps got louder as Jay started working his them in and out. She closed her eyes as pure pleasure engulfed her senses. Her mouth parted with the urge to scream but no sound erupted as she came hard all over Jay's face.

Jay kissed Shannon's drenched pussy one more time before retrieving the condom. After donning it, he moved over her trembling body, captivated by the rosy hue spiraling out over her body. She was so beautiful and he wanted to be inside her so badly. Jay positioned himself between her wet thighs and tapped the head of his cock on her clit. Shannon opened her eyes to meet his gaze.

"Take me." Her husky request elicited a gruff groan from Jay.

He pushed the head of his cock into her, pausing when Shannon gasped again. "I'll go slow."

Shannon nodded, lifting her knees up to her chest. "Give it to me. I want it all."

Jay gritted his teeth and sank a little deeper into her, pausing again when Shannon moaned.

"Yes." Shannon wriggled beneath him. "Don't stop."

Jay pressed forward, exhaling with the effort it took not to slam in balls deep. He admired Shannon's enthusiasm but he didn't want to hurt her. She was so snug. He slid back, pumping Shannon with shallow thrusts, observing her fingers gripping the sheets tighter.

"More, Jay. Give me more."

Jay swore—the minx was truly testing his mettle. "Red..." He pushed in a little deeper, groaning with pleasure when Shannon momentarily tightened the walls of her pussy around him.

"*More.*"

Her voice was all but a whisper, but her determination convinced Jay to move forward, little by little. When he'd given her all but an inch, Shannon cried out and dug her nails into back.

"Too much?" Jay kissed her nose, feeling his muscles burn with the restraint it took to keep most of his weight off her.

"Is that all of you?"

"No." Jay groaned when Shannon mouthed the word *more*. He obliged her, giving her all of him. Her shocked gasp made him harder. Jay bent his head and kissed her. He nipped her lip, raised his head to look at her face and waited for her dazed gaze to refocus on him before beginning to move. Jay savored the feel of her body beneath him, wrapped around him as he pumped her with easy, steady strokes. It was enough for him that she'd taken every inch.

"More."

"Minx."

Shannon's breathy demand as she bucked her hips beneath him was his undoing. He picked up his pace, riding her hard, holding nothing back. Pinpricks of pleasure started to converge into an all-consuming force that Jay no longer wanted to try to control.

"L-Let me taste." Shannon wet her bottom lip, gazing up at him with passion-glazed eyes. "I need to taste you."

Jay blinked at Shannon, realizing through the mind-numbing erotic haze fogging over his brain what she wanted. He pulled out of her and the action of removing the condom slowed his orgasm by seconds as he took his cock in hand. A bead of sweat trickled down his back as Shannon got on her knees.

"Feed me."

Her naughty request and the wicked sight of her parted, painted lips sent Jay over the edge. He came with another dark curse, making sure to give Shannon every bit of the taste she craved.

Chapter Five

Shannon accepted the glass of wine Jay held out to her. They both sipped in a companionable silence for a few moments, and Shannon was struck by how comfortable she felt with Jay. Granted they'd just had sex—amazing, hot sex—but a physical connection didn't always guarantee anything other than that. Shannon didn't feel the need to rush Jay off, neither did she sense he was in any hurry to leave.

A prickle of feminine awareness skittered over Shannon when Jay's jean-clad thigh brushed against her bare leg. She shifted a little on the soft cushion and sucked in a sharp breath at the pleasant twinges zinging between her legs.

"You okay?"

Shannon smiled. "I am." Her body ached but in a good way. She had been thoroughly taken, as she'd requested. Jay's passion had her feeling sated and happy. "Thank you for teaching me how to flip my omelet perfectly. You're a great teacher."

Jay wrapped his arm around her shoulder. "You're an adept student. More cooking lessons could be in your future."

"I hope so." Shannon took another drink from her glass. "Oh, this is nice."

"I thought you'd enjoy it. That wine we shared last night? Well, this bottle is from one of the boxes of bottled vino I brought back from that Napa Valley vineyard."

"I thought I liked the one I selected but I think this one is better." Shannon sighed. "It's the perfect finish to our meal."

Jay sat his glass on the table in front of them. "No" — he entangled his fingers in her hair, still damp from their shower earlier — "*you* are."

Shannon laughed as she lifted her face for his kiss. She moaned beneath his mouth, spellbound again by the way he moved his lips and tongue against hers. Her nipples pebbled beneath the short pink sundress she'd put on after her shower as she reached up to smooth her palms over his bare chest. She drew in a shuddering breath when he pulled away. "My goodness, but you're a damn good kisser."

Jay grinned. "Likewise." He caressed her cheek with his thumb.

"You know, I can't believe I'm with you right now."

"Why?"

Shannon shrugged. "We met…what, almost a month ago? Our dinner alone together…that kiss all happened by chance."

"I don't believe in chance." Jay reached for his wine again.

"You don't?"

"Nope." Jay finished a sip. "There are no coincidences in my opinion. We were supposed to have dinner alone and share a kiss that would leave us both wanting more."

Shannon giggled. "Wow. Okay. Well, I figured you weren't that into me when you didn't ask for my number or try to get in contact with me, being that we were at the same hotel before I left."

"I was just biding my time, didn't want to assume anything. I knew we'd meet again." Jay placed his hand on her thigh and the warmth of his touch sent a thrill through Shannon. "Red, I was attracted to you the moment I met you. I was glad Aimee decided to join her husband and leave the two of alone. We shared a good vibe from the beginning and that parting kiss? Well, it confirmed that I was going to have to seek you out for an official date once you returned for the taping of this show."

"Hmm. In a way, you'd say we were destined to be as we are right now?"

"Absolutely."

"Interesting." Shannon snuggled closer to Jay charmed by his words. He was an intriguing man.

"So, tell me something."

"Anything."

Jay toyed with her hair. "When you answered the door, you looked a little upset. What was going on right before I arrived?"

Shannon groaned. "I'd just got off the phone with my mum."

"You guys aren't close?"

"When my dad was alive to serve as a buffer, we were closer, but our relationship has always been complicated." Shannon sat up and reached for the bottle of wine on the table.

"All relationships are."

"Yes, well, ours makes me want to scream and cry at the same time, *all* the time." Shannon topped off her glass. "She just pushes too hard, has always wanted me to conform to her idea of who and what I should be and, as much as I hate to admit...I've given in to her way too many times."

"I see. So, you pushed back this evening and things went sideways."

"Try upside down." Shannon smiled when Jay chuckled. "I hate when we argue. Correction, when *I* argue. She always gets to be right and I'm always wrong. Anyways...what about you and Ari? Are you guys close to your parents?"

"Our parents died."

Shannon gasped. "Oh, I'm so sorry to hear that. At the same time?"

"Thanks. No, we didn't lose them at the same time. We lost our dad in car accident almost ten years ago." Jay released a breath. "Our mom lost her battle to breast cancer almost three years ago. Watching her fight for her life was one of the hardest things I've ever had to go through, something I hope I *never* have to deal with again."

"I'm sorry." Shannon placed her hand over Jay's, the pain in his voice welling up the need to comfort him in some small way. "That's a lot to deal with."

"It has been."

"I know you had to be strong for your sister for both tragedies."

Jay traced a line over her knuckles with his thumb. "We leaned on each other. I try to be there for Ari. Sometimes—most of the time—she can be a handful." Jay shook his head. "She's still finding her way. I've cut her a lot of slack on some things because of what we've had to deal with. I'm hoping her new job keeps her busy and out of the casinos."

"She likes to gamble?"

"Unfortunately." Jay grunted. "Ari is a bit of a thrill seeker." He groaned as his cell started to chime in a vibrant ringtone. "Speaking of Ari." Jay looked at Shannon. "I'm sorry. I've gotta take this call."

Shannon waved him on, watching him get up as he answered the call. She sipped her wine, reached for her phone to check her messages then groaned when she saw a text from her mum, requesting she call her tomorrow. Shannon had planned to take a day's reprieve from talking to her.

"Shannon, I have to go get Ari."

Shannon frowned as Jay sat his phone on the table. "Something wrong?"

"I'm not sure but she sounded funny on the phone, asked if I'd mind coming to get her." Jay grabbed his shirt and pulled it over his head. "She usually doesn't want me around when she's out, thinks I mess up her vibe with potential dates."

"You're protective of her." Shannon stood as Jay stuffed his phone into his jeans pocket. "I wish I had a big brother like you. I hope everything is okay." She walked with him to the door.

"Me too." Jay slipped his feet into his leather thongs. He wrapped his arms around her. "I'm sorry I have to leave so soon."

"Me too." Shannon grinned as Jay smiled. "Please text or call me later and let me know your sister is all right."

"I will." Jay gave her a quick kiss as he opened the door. "Later, Red."

"Later." Shannon pushed the door closed then leaned against it with a blissful sigh.

It had been a perfect evening. Great conversation, food and sex. Her body still thrummed from Jay's touch. The dull throb between her legs made her squeeze her inner thighs together. Shannon drew in a sharp breath when her action sent off tiny aftershocks of tender pleasure within her. Tendrils of heat licked up her spine as she recalled the intense, erotic sensations of ecstasy and pain that had enveloped her when Jay had finally done as she'd repeatedly asked and pushed his cock in to the hilt.

Shannon moved away from the door with a little shiver and a small smile. She wondered how soon she could ask Jay for another cooking lesson, because she knew exactly what would be on the menu.

* * * *

Jay strode inside the Egyptian-themed hotel, scanning the lobby for his sister. It had taken him exactly twenty-three minutes to get to her. His mind had been racing with all the possible reasons for her ringing him. The place was packed with people enjoying the sights, sounds and food the popular spot was known for. Jay breathed a sigh of relief when he spotted Ari in the crowd. She'd changed into a long, slinky magenta dress that was deceptively demure at first glance. His sister's midriff was exposed and the slit along the skirt showed off her legs. Jay gritted his teeth. His sister's antics were going to be the death of him, and who was that man she chatting with? Jay took a few steps in her direction then frowned. *Ryder?*

As if sensing his presence, Ari lifted her head, met his gaze and her smile faltered for a split second before she offered an even wider one. Yup, something had definitely gone down.

"Hi, Ryder."

Ryder tilted his head in his direction. "Jay."

"Hey, Jay." Ari glanced at Ryder. "We were just talking about you. Well, not you, the show —"

"Ari, what's going on?" Jay hated it when she rambled to avoid saying what she needed to say. "On the phone it sounded like something was going on."

"What? No." Ari wrapped her arms around her exposed midriff. "I just thought I could share a celebratory drink with my brother for a job well done after your first night on television."

Jay looked at Ryder, who was staring at his sister with the same what-the-fuck expression that had to be on his face. "Oh, really?"

Ari nodded. "Yep."

"You two should celebrate. The premiere was great." Ryder cast a glance between them. "I'm going to call it a night." He offered his hand to Jay, shaking it before turning to Ari. "Ari, I'm glad I ran into you. You have an amazing voice."

"Thank you, Ryder." Ari continued to avoid making eye contact with Jay. "Good night."

"Night."

Both Jay and Ari watched him stride toward the exit. One bulky man flanked his side and Jay assumed it was his bodyguard from the way he carried himself. Jay shifted his attention to Ari and found her looking at him, her expression unreadable. "Are you okay?"

"I'm fine. I shouldn't have called you. I know you had plans."

"Ari, I know you and you wouldn't have called unless something was wrong. Did your call have something to do with Ryder? Was he — ?"

"Ryder was a perfect gentleman. He saw me and I guess decided to keep me company as I waited for you."

Jay raised an eyebrow. "How did he get to hear you sing?"

"See that piano over there?" Ari pointed to the gleaming black baby grand roped off in a corner of the plush lobby. "Well, Ryder has permission to play it whenever he wants. He's got connections. Did you know he could play?"

"No, Ari."

"He can. I mean he can *really* play. I went over to listen, asked him if I could sing with him and I did."

"Cool."

Ari grinned. "It was. The lobby practically froze for a moment while we did our thing. It was so amazing. The highlight of my crazy evening."

"So, something else did happen?"

"Yes. I got all dressed up and my date canceled. I was feeling lonely and bored, decided to call you. That's what happened. No big deal, okay?"

Jay studied her, not even half convinced he was getting the full story.

"Look"—Ari tugged at his arm—"can we just go? I'm hungry. Did you already eat?"

Flashes of Shannon's long legs draped over his shoulders as he'd feasted on her popped into his mind as he nodded. "I did, but let's go get something. Wanna eat here?"

"No." Ari looked around them. "Let's go somewhere a little less crowded."

"Okay." Jay led them toward the exit, deciding to press more details from Ari about her evening later.

"So" — Ari linked her arm with his as they stepped outside into the balmy night air — "how was *your* night? I *know* I called you at an inopportune time."

Jay scoffed. "You aren't sharing details of your night, so you'll get none of the particulars of mine."

"Fine." Ari pretended to pout but Jay knew she was relieved to be off the hook. "Can we go to that one place with the sushi?"

"You paying?"

"Next week."

Jay shook his head with a wry grin. "Right."

"No, really." Ari gave him a look that said she was serious.

"Okay. What did you sing with Ryder?"

"*As Time Goes By*." Ari squealed. "Jay, I rocked it. I totally rocked it."

Jay congratulated his sister again, content to tune out the rest of her conversation. His thoughts were on Shannon and the incredible night they'd shared together. He'd enjoyed talking with her, cooking with her…and fucking her. Well, taking Red had to be at the top of his blissful moments when it came to having sex. He hadn't been with many women who could take all of him and he sure as hell hadn't been with a woman eager to swallow. Shannon had practically begged for him to come in her mouth. "Fuck."

"Excuse me? Jay? Are you listening to me?"

Jay looked at his sister, realizing he'd cursed out loud. "I heard you."

"Uh huh. What did I just say?"

Jay smiled. "You were talking about singing with Ryder and how well it went."

"Uh huh. You didn't hear a damn thing I just said." Ari playfully punched him. "You must've had *some* evening."

"Likewise, little sis, likewise."

Ari cleared her throat. "Anyways...*pay* attention. There will be questions following."

Jay chuckled as his sister started to tell her story all over again. It took more effort than he thought it would to concentrate on what she was saying. He kept getting distracted by the look of pure ecstasy on Shannon's face when he'd pushed balls deep inside her. Christ, he couldn't wait to see her, to feel and taste her again.

It had been almost a year since his last serious relationship and he hadn't missed the emotional ties and energy required to maintain one. He'd focused on getting his career off the ground and that had been enough, but now?

Jay exhaled, managing to nod at the appropriate moment when Ari glanced his way. He didn't know if he wanted a serious relationship but he did know he wanted more of Shannon, and if he didn't watch it, she could easily become a craving. Jay only hoped he'd stirred up the same need in her.

* * * *

"Hey, Shannon."

Shannon turned to see Misha Banner approaching her with a cooing baby in her arms. "Hello, Misha. It's been a while. Wow! Is that your daughter?" It was only a cursory question—the little girl resembled her mother and Cameron.

"Yes." Misha grinned, her pretty face alight with joy. "This is Sia."

Shannon smiled. "She's beautiful."

"Thank you." Misha nuzzled Sia. "I didn't get a chance to say hello last night. It's good to see you."

"You as well." Shannon tugged on Sia's cute onesie. "I'm so glad you decided to be a judge for the show."

"I was concerned about disrupting things for Sia at first, but she's such an easy-going baby. Cameron convinced me she would be fine if I brought her and he was right." Misha kissed Sia's cheek then gestured around the bustling set. "She doesn't seem to mind all the action or noise around here."

"How's the rest of the family?"

"Crazy, but good." Misha chuckled. "Serene's son, Sam, is a handful, likes to breastfeed around the clock."

Shannon chuckled, ignoring twinges of jealousy as Misha brought up her phone and proceeded to show her an adorable picture of Serene's baby boy. It was times like this that Shannon wished she had something other than work going on in her life. "Sam has his daddy's eyes."

"I know, right?" Misha switched Sia to her other arm. "Anyway, I can't tell you how weird it is to see Cameron and Oliver bouncing babes and talking diapers."

"I bet. I'm so happy for you guys."

"Thanks, Shannon." Misha frowned as her daughter whined. "I better go feed her before I run out of time. Are you going to Ryder's impromptu cast and crew party tonight?"

"I'll probably pop in for a little bit. You?"

Misha shook her head. "No. Sia and I have a Skype date with Daddy."

"Aww…how nice."

"Well, I'll see you out there." Misha giggled. "The competition is going to be fierce tonight. I can't wait for the secret ingredient to be revealed to Kelly, Oscar and Jay."

"I know." Shannon wiggled Sia's tiny foot. "All right, then."

"Bye."

Shannon waved to Sia as Misha pivoted. She headed to her dressing room to change, disappointed she hadn't run into Jay. He'd texted her last night to say good night and inform her Ari was fine. Shannon had wanted to hear his voice. Her morning had flown by with two interviews, thanks to Aimee and Shawn's relentless PR schedule. Shannon checked her phone for new messages, sighing when there was one from everyone apart from the name she wanted to see.

"There you are."

Shannon's pulse quickened in response to Jay's voice before she lifted her head to see him standing by her dressing room. "Hey." She drank in the sight of him in his chef uniform. The white fabric was a striking contrast against his skin. Shannon resisted the urge to touch him as she pictured his muscled body beneath. Shannon wet her bottom lip, remembering the taste of him on her tongue, and tiny circles of desire spiraled within her.

Jay smiled. "Hey. I was hoping to see you before the show started. How are you?"

"I'm okay." Shannon wished his polite question hadn't filled her mind with erotic flashbacks of their sexual interlude. She smiled at a production assistant passing by, conscious of her body language and the other people milling around them too. Shannon realized they hadn't discussed whether or not they were going to openly see one another. "How are you? Ready for round two?" Shannon silently cursed the color she knew was flooding her cheeks but heaven help her, *she* was ready for round two right now.

Jay took a step closer to her and the air between seemed to electrify even more. "Damn right, I am." He gestured to her clothes. "You don't look ready though."

"I'm going to change now." Shannon smoothed a hand over her orange sundress. "What do you think of this shade of orange on me?"

Jay's gaze flicked over her, lingering on her breasts. "I like it." He stuffed his hands into his pants, drawing Shannon's attention to the unmistakable imprint of his hard-on. "A lot."

"Thanks." Shannon smiled, arousal sending a rush of heat through her.

"I should go."

Shannon glanced around the momentarily empty hallway then opened the door to her dressing room. "Don't go yet." She stepped inside, aware of Jay coming in behind her. Shannon turned to face him as he closed the door.

Jay snaked his arm around her and brought her in close to his body. "You know this isn't a good idea. We go live in—"

"I don't care." Shannon lifted her face for his kiss and was rewarded. She melted against him as he crushed his mouth to hers. Shannon moaned as Jay deepened the kiss, loving the feel of his hands on her ass as he pressed her against his thick cock. She pulled away breathless, wanting more. "I'm hungry, Jay."

"I left you hungry?" Jay reached out and caressed her breast, setting off delicious tingles within her. "That's unacceptable."

Shannon gave him a wicked smile, recognizing his familiar question and response. "Yes, it is." She brought her hand up to his pants, reveling in his sharp intake of air as she unzipped them and slipped her hand inside to pull out his cock. She caressed him as she squatted and looked up at him. "Are you going to feed me?"

"Fuck, yes."

Chapter Six

Jay clenched his jaw as Shannon swirled her tongue around the head of his cock. Her soft moan of appreciation made him harder as she took him into her mouth. "Damn, woman."

Shannon responded by taking hold of his thighs. Jay caressed her scalp as she worked him in and out of her mouth faster. He pushed his fingers into her hair, content to let her set the pace.

"Mmm." Shannon briefly lifted her face to his, a sultry smile on her wet lips. "I can't get enough of the taste of you."

Jay grunted as she kissed the tip of his dick then took him deep into her throat. He felt the same way about her. "Jesus." It took way too much effort to utter that one word. Jay tightened his grip in her hair, the need to come taking over every other rational thought. He relished the wicked warmth of Shannon's lips wrapped around him, didn't think he'd ever been with a woman so giving when it came to oral sex. "Shannon…"

Saying her name was the only way he could warn her to pull back. Jay swore again when Shannon reinvigorated her already impressive effort to please him. Swept up with the intensity of the climax claiming his senses, Jay took over feeding his cock to Shannon. He thrust deeply into her throat, groaning as he came. He tried to suppress the shudders tearing through his body as Shannon hungrily swallowed every bit of what he had to offer.

Shannon took her mouth off him then gently squeezed the head of his cock, as if to milk him dry. "Delicious." She placed another soft kiss on him.

Jay found Shannon's husky voice almost as endearing as her flushed face. He pulled her up, pushed her up against the door and glided his hand beneath her dress. "You're delicious." Jay slipped his hand into her lace panties, smiling when he discovered just how wet she was. He teased her clit, kissing her when she moaned. "We don't have time for what I'd really like to do to you." Jay pressed his palm on Shannon's clit, enjoying her ragged groan as he slid two fingers inside her. He nipped her neck as she lifted her leg, giving him better access. Her juices soaked his hand as he finger-fucked her, and Jay kept kissing her to keep the sexy noises she was making from carrying through the door.

"Faster."

Shannon's whispered demand was exactly what he wanted to do. He hooked his fingers, picking up his relaxed pace within her when she tightened her sheath around his slick fingers.

"Faster, Jay."

Jay obliged her, tunneling in and out of her at record speed. He braced his leg between Shannon's as she wobbled against him. Jay smiled when her pussy quivered around his fingers and she came with a muffled cry. He continued to stroke her, slowing his pace before gently removing his hand from between her wet thighs.

"I-I can't believe how quickly you made me come." Shannon's breath was hot against his neck.

"Likewise." Jay brought his fingers up to his mouth.

"Let me taste too."

Jay chuckled as he offered his hand to Shannon. "Haven't you had enough yet, Red?"

"No. You?" Shannon's sassy smile delighted him.

"No, and I'm glad to hear that you agree because after the show —"

"*After* the show we have the weekend to satisfy our insatiable appetites." Shannon dragged the tip of her tongue up his palm. "Think that'll be enough time?"

Jay started to answer as someone knocked on the door.

"Erby, you in there?"

Shannon's eyes widened as she mouthed the name, "Ryder."

Jay nodded, wondering how much of their conversation had carried through the door.

"Shannon?" Ryder's voice was laced with impatience.

"Yes?" Shannon called out over Jay's shoulder.

"Shawn wants a word with us before the show starts. Meet in twenty minutes?"

"Okay."

Both remained silent for a few moments.

"Do you think he heard anything?" Shannon moved from his embrace, quickly stripping out of her sundress.

"I don't think so." Jay stuffed his semi-erect cock back into his pants and zipped up. "Are you going to be able to get dressed in enough time?"

Shannon grinned. "I'm a pro at this. I'll be down to makeup in less than eight minutes." She took a step forward and kissed him on the lips. "Good luck out there tonight. I'll be rooting for you."

"Let me have" — Jay tugged on her emerald panties — "*these* for good luck."

"Mmm. I'm not sure I have an extra pair here."

"Good." Jay squeezed her ass then released her. "I like the idea of knowing you're bare beneath your dress for me."

"So do I." Shannon wriggled out of her panties and handed the damp fabric to him.

Jay grinned as he pocketed them. He opened the door to her dressing room, took a peek, found the coast clear then stepped out. "Later, Red."

"Later."

Jay smiled when Shannon blew him a kiss as he shut her door. He headed over to his station, making a concentrated effort not to smile like a fool. Shannon made him feel like a high-school teenager giddy over gaining the attention from the prettiest girl in class.

"What are you grinning about?" Kelly narrowed her gaze at him as he approached the cooking stations. "Did you overhear what the secret ingredient is or something?"

Jay chuckled, amused that his efforts to hide his happiness had failed. "Nope. Just excited to see what they throw our way this round."

"You should both prepare yourselves to go home." Oscar tapped an oversized fork on his countertop. "I haven't encountered an ingredient yet I couldn't cook the hell out of."

"Oscar, you might wanna put that mega-sized horn you're tooting on over there away before things get underway." Kelly flashed a derisive smile Jay's way as he laughed. She tucked a blue-streaked lock behind her ear with little sigh. "I think I'm actually going to squeal with delight when you're chopped. I might even come from behind this station and do a little dance on national television."

Oscar chuckled. "I wonder if your food has as much punch as your words."

"Oh, did I bruise that enormous ego of yours, Chef Blithe?" Kelly waved an oven mitten in his direction.

"Hey. There's no need to take out the knives just yet, you two." Jay grinned at both chefs starting at him. "May the best chef win tonight."

Oscar saluted them. "That's me."

Jay shook his head as Oscar and Kelly went at it again. He reached in his pocket to retrieve his vibrating cell while patting the other one that contained Shannon's pretty panties. Jay unlocked the device and read the incoming text from Ari.

Isn't this dress perfect for my debut this week?

Ari quickly sent an accompanying photo of her wearing a slinky red number that hit mid-thigh. Jay groaned as he responded.

How much do you need, Ari?

His sister's reply came back a nanosecond later.

Borrow, big brother. Two hundred dollars?

Jay hit the keys on his phone as a production assistant announced the taping was about to begin.

Use my card. I'm taking it back when I see you later.

He grinned when all he got back from Ari was a smiley face. It was hard to get annoyed over his sister's request. He was too damned pleased.

Jay's gaze drifted over to Shannon as she entered the set, lovely in royal blue sheath dress that swished around her legs. As if knowing she was being observed, Shannon turned her head. She looked at him, her expression neutral, but Jay caught the sparkle in her eyes. A curious euphoria surged through Jay as Shannon greeted the studio audience, confirming he had it bad for the spicy redhead.

* * * *

Supremely conscious of her nakedness beneath her dress, Shannon suppressed a tiny shiver alongside Ryder. She was eager to hear the results for this round of the competition but more so to finally be alone with Jay once more. Shannon suppressed a tiny shiver of delight as she glanced at him again and her heart skipped a beat when she met his heated gaze. It took effort not to smile at an inappropriate time as she focused on her job.

Shannon hoped Jay's culinary skills hadn't faltered due to the distracting thoughts, because she'd struggled more than once to read the teleprompter without any hitches. Thank goodness they were at the end of the show. "Well, Ryder, I think our chefs had their work cut out for them with the secret ingredient for their dishes being coconut."

Ryder nodded. "Indeed, Shannon, but doesn't it smell delicious in here?"

"It does." Shannon beamed at Ryder.

"But one of these fine chef's didn't make the cut." Ryder shrugged as the crowd booed. "I know it's sad but that's how this competition works, folks. So, which entree didn't deliver? Is it Kelly's blackened salmon with crunchy coconut couscous?"

"Or Oscar's beer-battered coconut shrimp with his savory strawberry arugula salad?" Shannon added as the audience murmured with excitement. "Perhaps Jay's coconut chicken with Gruyere potatoes? It's all up to our judges."

Shannon shifted her gaze over the panel of judges. "Have you reached a decision, judges?"

"We have." Misha's smile was warm. "It was a tough to decide who to chop when each chef presented us with a scrumptious dish. In the end, it came down to layers of flavor. Chef Myer, we've collectively agreed the flavor of your salmon didn't completely complement your crunchy coconut couscous. I'm sorry, Chef Myer, but..." Misha paused as the audience seemed to collectively gasp. "You've been cut."

Ryder groaned along with the crowd. "Wait. There is still a chance for Chef Myer, right Shannon?"

"That's correct, Ryder. This is an exciting change in the format for *Celeb Hotel Chef* that can only come into play when we get down to the last three players. The judges can offer a chopped chef the chance to redeem themselves by taking part in a cook-off challenge. The chopped chef gets to challenge one of the remaining two chefs and if Chef Myer were to win—"

"She would proceed to the final showdown and her challenger would be the one leaving the show." Ryder held out his hand to the judges. "Esteemed panel, are you giving Chef Myer the chance to stay?"

The audience went wild when Don Mackey began vigorously nodding his head. "Yes, we are, Ryder."

"Congratulations, Chef Myer." Shannon walked over to a tearful Kelly, giving her a second to clear her throat before speaking. "Who would you like to challenge?"

"Chef Blithe," Kelly answered without a moment's hesitation, and thunderous clapping ensued as Shannon turned to the cameras.

"There you have it." Shannon moved to stand next to Ryder. "Join us next week for the cook-off challenge between Chef Myer and Chef Blithe."

"Good night, everybody." Ryder waved and Shannon did the same, both waiting to move until after the red lights above the cameras turned off. "Great show, Erby," Ryder paused as a production assistant hurried over to retrieve their hand held mics. "Great show, considering."

"Considering what?" Shannon frowned when Ryder flashed a sardonic grin.

"Considering how distracted you were." Ryder held up his hand when she parted her lips to speak. "Oh, I'm sure no one else noticed. I probably wouldn't have unless..."

"Unless what?" Shannon couldn't mask the irritation in her voice as Ryder leaned in close.

"Unless I hadn't stopped by your dressing room earlier. Next time, move away from the door. Don't worry, I won't tell a soul about you and Jay Dax."

Shannon gaped at Ryder, her cheeks burning as he winked at her then walked off. She stared at his retreating form in shock and embarrassment, trying to decide whether she wanted to go after him and give him a piece of her mind or let it go. "Of all the damn nerve."

The man was unconscionable but she had decided she liked him. He could've said something much nastier or exploited her personal affairs. Shannon exhaled as Shawn appeared on set. She couldn't wait to talk to Jay.

"Cast and crew, your attention please." Shawn waited until everyone around him quieted. "I'd like to invite you all to join me tonight at the Banner restaurant for free food and drinks. I'm proud of how well *Celeb Hotel Chef* is doing ratings-wise. You all deserve a pat on the back for a job well done." Shawn held up his hand to stem the applause. "Come tonight. Party starts at ten o'clock. Oh, and whoever doesn't show up? Is fired." Shawn grinned at the good-natured grumbling before walking off.

Shannon sighed. Going to Shawn's impromptu party wasn't exactly how she wanted to spend the rest of her evening. No, she wanted to spend it with Jay. Shannon bit her bottom lip as she sought him out, imagining herself with her legs wrapped around his muscled torso. God, he was the best lover she'd ever had—he made her feel things she'd never felt before, and the taste of him…? She didn't think she'd ever get enough.

Shannon waved to members of the crew, her heels clacking loudly on the floor as she headed over to Jay, still standing at his station talking to Kelly. "Kelly, I wish you well in your challenge against Oscar next week."

"Thanks." Kelly chuckled. "Are you going to give the same well wishes to Oscar?"

"Of course." Shannon smiled. "I have to remain impartial and diplomatic, no matter whom I'd choose to win."

Kelly beamed, clearly getting Shannon's unspoken sentiment. "Gotcha. Well, I'm going to change and relax before tonight's shindig. Maybe I'll even find a pretty lady to come with me."

Shannon chuckled as she retreated, shifting her attention to Jay. "Congratulations, Chef Dax. You did exceptionally well this time."

Jay came from around his station, his gaze never leaving hers. "Are we talking about my cooking skills?"

"Among other things."

Jay nodded. "Hmm. Well, thank you." He glanced at his watch. "Looks like we have approximately an hour and a half before our presence is required at Tempted."

"Is that enough time?" Shannon didn't think it was, especially when all she could think about was coming over and over again with his thick cock deep inside her pussy.

"Depends."

"On?" Shannon searched Jay's face for the answer, astounded by the seemingly unquenchable streak of desire zipping through her. She wanted to close the gap between them regardless of the other people around them.

"Well" — Jay followed her toward the dressing rooms — "I'd imagine it depends on how many times you'd like to come before that party."

"Mmm…one more time would suffice." Shannon glanced around them as they walked, making sure no one was overhearing their naughty conversation.

"Really?" Jay raised his eyebrow at her.

Shannon shrugged. "There's always tomorrow."

"Hmm." Jay held her gaze. "And would that be with my mouth, my hands or my cock?"

Jay's barely whispered question made her nipples pebble. "I'll leave that up to you."

"My room or yours?"

"Yours." Shannon figured that was only fair, given the last time they were together.

"All right." Jay stopped by her dressing room door. "I'll see you in about a half hour."

"Okay." Shannon watched him depart before twisting the handle beneath her grasp. She stepped inside, closed the door then braced her body against it. "Don't fall for him." Shannon stared at her reflection in the mirror, her pulse quickening as she envisioned Jay bringing her to such a sweet orgasm a short while ago in the same spot. She was in real danger of doing something foolish, something like falling for a man who obviously liked sleeping with her but had shown no evidence he wanted to share anything more than great sex with her.

Her cell chimed, drawing her attention to her dresser. Shannon crossed over to it and picked the device up to see a reminder from her calendar. She needed to make an appointment with her gynecologist for her annual checkup. "Damn." She'd put it off twice already. Now she was out of state and she needed a new prescription for birth control. Like it or not, she was going to have to find a local doctor and go.

Shannon grabbed her purse and sifted through its contents to find her contraceptive packet. She opened it and sighed. Four pills left. At any other time, she'd put off going to the doctor but that wasn't an option at the present moment—not with Jay in the picture. As much as she hated the idea of going, Shannon set a reminder on her phone to find and call a doctor tomorrow. She set the device down just as it started to chime again to alert her of her mother's incoming call. "Double damn," Shannon muttered as she answered. "Hello, Mum. How are you?"

"I'm well. You certainly looked well tonight. Your cheeks were a pretty rose color during the entire show. New blush?"

Shannon exhaled, noting how her mother hadn't actually asked how *she* was doing. "I think it was. I'd have to ask Shelly."

"Shelly always knows how to bring out the color of your eyes. I'm glad you've been able to keep the same makeup artist for so long."

Shannon took off one earring. "Me too. It's too bad you don't appreciate Anna's talent as my stylist like you do Shelly."

"Let's not get into that subject again. I called for a specific reason."

Shannon rolled her eyes as her mother cleared her throat. She *always* called for a specific reason.

"You know, the last time we talked I didn't get a chance to tell you about my surprise."

"Ah, yes." Shannon shifted her phone to her other ear and took off her other earring. "Well, don't keep me in suspense, Mother. What's the surprise?"

"I'm flying out for the last taping of your show."

Shannon dropped the dangly hoop in her grasp as her mum continued.

"I'll be in Vegas for two nights! Isn't this exciting?"

"Wow." Shannon bent to pick up her jewelry, trying to think of the exact phrase that would impart a thrill she didn't feel. "This *is* a surprise."

"I knew you didn't think I'd come." Clarion chuckled, obviously pleased with herself. "I can't wait to see what all the fuss is about for that wild city and I'm looking forward to seeing you work live again."

"Will you be staying at the Banner Hotel?" Shannon sat in the chair in front of her vanity, rested her head on her hand and wondered how she was going to survive two full days in her mom's company.

"Of course. I booked a room with a fabulous view of The Strip."

"Anything in particular you'd like to see or do?" Shannon tossed her earring next to its match on the table.

"I know you're busy and my trip is last minute." Clarion hesitated, as if she wanted Shannon to counter her statement with some fluffy reassurances. "I'd love to catch a live show with that one singer I'm always talking about."

"Okay." Shannon knew tickets for that show would be pricey but she didn't mind. It meant at least one night would be occupied with something for them to do other than talk.

"Oh, and I'd love to meet your co-host. Perhaps we could all have dinner?"

Shannon blew out breath. "Mother, whatever you're thinking...squash it. I'd be happy to introduce you to Ryder but I'm not going to make plans with him just so you can play matchmaker."

"Fine. I've got to go. My bridge partners are here. I'll send you my flight itinerary later this evening."

"All right. Have fun."

"Will do."

Shannon didn't bother saying goodbye, knowing her mum had already hung up. She ended the call with a heavy heart. Her mother seemed to have an uncanny knack in ruining her mood. Shannon looked at herself in the mirror. She slipped off her shoes with a little sigh. She wished she didn't always have her guard up when she talked to her mum, wished that she could talk to her about anything—like her unexpected burgeoning feelings for Jay.

A stab of pain pierced Shannon's heart when she considered his interest in her was purely sexual. Her high-profile job got her noticed but oddly enough didn't get her many dates and the ones she did get…well, it became clear sex and status was the name of the game. Shannon stood up and shrugged out of her outfit. She was tired of playing the dating game, tired of being disappointed.

Shannon hung the dress on a rack crammed with other options she could've worn. She reached for the sundress she'd come in, thinking about her mother and her disastrous track record with the opposite sex. Shannon sniffed back tears as she contemplated the possibility there was something about her…something that kept the ones she loved from loving her back the way she needed.

Chapter Seven

Jay searched the Banner restaurant for Shannon, greeting people as he weaved his way through the crowd to the bar. Something was up. He'd been surprised to get Shannon's text informing him she'd meet him at the party. That hadn't been the original plan. He'd been looking forward to spending time with her, touching and kissing her again. It was those yearnings that had kept him hard as he'd showered.

"How do you not have a drink in hand?" Kelly giggled, as she lifted her beer for a sip.

"I just got here." Jay smiled at the buxom brunette by the chef's side.

"Jay, this is Vicki." Kelly wrapped her arm around the lady. "Vicki, Jay."

"Nice to meet you, Vicki." Jay nodded at Bret, a bartender he'd hired when he'd taken the position as executive chef for the classy restaurant.

"What can I get you, boss?"

"Scotch, neat." Jay gestured behind Bret. "How are things going back there?"

"Channelle has things under control." Bret leaned in close. "I think she's got her eye on your job."

Jay chuckled. "Oh, I know."

"Hey, Jay."

Jay turned to see Shannon standing behind him. "Hey." He resisted the urge to snake his arm around her waist and yank her to his side. They hadn't discussed whether their relationship was public or private. *Hell, does she even consider what we have as a relationship?* Jay drank in the sight of her as she greeted Kelly and Vicki. She looked amazing, dressed in a pair of tight dark jeans and a shimmering top that hung off one shoulder. "How are you?" Jay asked when she turned her attention back to him. He decided her liked seeing her dressed casually as much as he enjoyed seeing her decked out in jewels and fancy dresses.

Shannon shrugged. "Okay. You?"

"Concerned."

"Concerned?" Shannon took a step closer to him as someone passed behind her. "Why?"

"Because your smile doesn't match the light in your eyes." Jay thanked Bret for his drink then looked at Shannon. "What are you drinking?"

"White wine." Shannon smiled at Bret as he nodded and walked off.

"I was looking forward to seeing you before this thing jumped off." Jay glanced at the handful of dancers that had taken to the floor in the center of the restaurant.

"I'm sorry." Shannon tossed her loose hair over one shoulder. "I know that's not what we discussed earlier."

"Well, you're here now and I'm glad. You look fantastic, by the way."

Shannon smoothed a hand over her jeans. "Really?" She accepted her drink from Bret with a friendly smile before looking at Jay. "This isn't my usual look but I didn't feel like dressing up."

"I like you dressed down." Jay leaned in close to her, so what he had to say wouldn't be overheard. "I like you even better naked and trembling beneath me." His words had the desired effect. Jay grinned as Shannon's eyes widened. Jay wanted to kiss the blush highlighting her cheeks as she sipped from her glass. "Dance with me?"

"Oh, no." Shannon waved her hand, taking another drink. "I don't really dance."

Jay took her by the hand. "You don't have to. All you have to do is follow my lead, Red."

Shannon took a generous sip from her glass. "I don't know —"

Jay didn't wait for her to finish. He gently pulled her toward the circular dance floor, aware of her fingers squeezing his as they joined the others enjoying the slow jam that had begun to play. Jay took Shannon into his arms and languidly swayed to the beat of the music, content at last. He felt her relax against him, following his lead with the ease and grace he'd expected. "You lied."

"What?" Shannon lifted her head from his chest to look at him.

"You do know how to dance."

Shannon grinned. "You're doing all the work. Leave me out here alone and I promise you, I wouldn't have a clue what to do."

"You'd just shake this gorgeous body of yours to the beat." Jay bent his head to breathe in the familiar scent of her hair. "I'd love to see you dance...alone."

"Like a stripper?" Shannon stiffened against him.

"No, like my woman putting on a sexy show just for me to enjoy." Jay pulled back a little to look down at her, detecting a tone in her voice. "Shannon, what's wrong?"

Shannon shook her head. "I'm sorry."

"That's the second time you've apologized but I'm not sure what you're apologizing for." Jay held her more loosely to see her face. "Did I do something to upset you?"

Shannon squeezed him. "You haven't done anything. I'm just a little discombobulated. My mum informed me earlier she's coming to visit and honestly, I'm not looking forward to having her here. We're better with each other when we've got some distance between us."

"Ah. I know you said you two don't always see eye to eye. How long will she stay?"

"Two nights."

Jay chuckled. "You can survive two nights, right?"

"I suppose."

"I can relate to family getting on my nerves, trust me. Ari can push my buttons sometimes and I didn't always get along with our dad, but I'd give anything for a little more time with him, rocky or not."

"You're right." Shannon gave him a bright smile. "I'm going to try to make the best of it."

Jay hoped he hadn't offended Shannon as the song they were dancing to faded out and live piano music filled the space. People started walking off the dance floor toward the baby grand located by the bar. Curious to see who was playing, Jay guided Shannon in that direction. It wasn't the night for the musician who normally had a set. Jay was surprised to see Ryder tinkling the ivories.

"Wow. I knew Ryder had a background in music but I wasn't aware he could play." Shannon tugged on Jay's hand. "And look, I think your sister is going to sing."

"I didn't know she was coming tonight." Jay had told her about the party, expecting her to plead her case for crashing it, but she hadn't seemed interested. Now it appeared she'd come to the party with Ryder. Jay wanted to know exactly what was going on between the two.

A hush came over the crowd as Ari step forward with a mic in hand, radiant in a lime dress he hadn't seen before. She nodded at Ryder, who began playing the intro to a tune Jay instantly recognized as *The Look of Love*. He watched his sister, proud of her poise and tone as she started to sing the romantic classic.

"She's good," Shannon whispered, giving him what seemed like the first genuine smile of the evening.

"She is." Jay cast his gaze between Ari and Ryder as they performed, impressed by them both. His sister knew how to engage the crowd with her smile and body movements. He clapped along with everyone else when Ryder brought the song to a dramatic close.

"They were both fantastic." Shannon placed her hand on Jay's arm. "Let's go over and congratulate them."

Jay walked with Shannon toward the piano and Ari rushed over to them with a delighted laugh. "Great job, Ari."

"Yes, you were terrific." Shannon shook her head. "I can't believe you haven't been performing on stage somewhere already."

"Thank you, you guys." Ari gave them both a quick hug. "I was so nervous."

"Didn't look like it." Jay tilted his head in Ryder's direction when the man made eye contact. "You and Ryder did a helluva job."

Shannon nodded. "I'm going to go tell Ryder the same thing."

Jay waited until Shannon walked off to speak. "What are you doing here, little sister? I mentioned this party to you and you seemed less than interested."

"I changed my mind." Ari toyed with the necklace around her neck. "You sorta mentioned I could come."

"Did you come with Ryder? What's going on with you two?"

"I did come with him." Ari briefly glanced at Ryder. "What? You don't approve?"

"Approve of what, exactly?"

His sister sighed. "Ryder's fun and he's mad talented. He called me, invited me to the party and suggested we perform a song together. I couldn't resist. This was great practice for my debut performance tomorrow night. Speaking of tomorrow night... You're going to be there, right?"

"Of course." Jay searched Ari's face. "Are you and Ryder—?"

Ari placed her hand on his chest. "I don't ask you about your sex life, do I? Please, please, don't ask me about mine."

Jay raised an eyebrow, but didn't press the issue any further with his sister. His gaze shifted to Ryder as the man walked toward him with Shannon. He'd talk to Ryder. He'd have no problem doing that.

"Your sister has an amazing gift." Ryder shook Jay's hand.

"And so do you." Jay released the man's hand, quelling the need to put his hand around his throat and demand his intentions where his sister was concerned. "I'm surprised you never pursued a career in music as an artist."

Ryder waved his hand. "I've always questioned whether or not to pursue music from that angle. Sometimes, like tonight, I wonder what might've been if I had of concentrated on my own music instead of producing songs for others."

"Well, it's not too late. You possess the charisma and the skill to have a phenomenal career as a musician."

Ryder grinned at Shannon. "Thank you, Erby. I appreciate you saying that."

"I think a drink is in order to celebrate our smashing performance together." Ari linked her arm with Ryder's.

"Absolutely." Ryder looked at Jay and Shannon. "Care to join us?"

Jay glanced at Shannon who nodded. "Sure. Lead the way." He placed his hand on the small of Shannon's back as they all moved toward the bar, wondering at the exact nature of his relationship with Shannon and Ari's with Ryder.

* * * *

Shannon drew in a deep breath as she glanced around the sterile doctor's office. She wished she were any place else as a soft knock drew her attention to the door slowly opening.

A petite brunette with a gentle smile entered. "Good afternoon, Shannon. I'm Doctor Calvin."

Shannon shook Doctor Calvin's offered hand. "Hello."

"I understand you are in need of a birth control prescription?"

"Yes." Shannon straightened her posture as the doctor approached with her stethoscope. "I've been putting off my annual because of work."

Doctor Calvin nodded. "I understand. No one really wants to come in for these visits. It's hard to make something you don't really want to do a priority. Lie back for me?"

Shannon did as the doctor commanded, appreciating the woman's warmth.

"I'll do your annual and a breast exam today. We'll get you out of here with the prescription you need in no time, okay?"

"Okay."

"Have you been experiencing anything out of the norm in regards to your health?" Doctor Calvin gently slipped her hand beneath her paper gown and Shannon concentrated on a spot on the ceiling as the doctor touched her breast.

"Other than being exceptionally tired and a little more nauseous than usual during my cycle, no." Shannon tried to remain still as the doctor continued her examination.

"Any tenderness here?"

Shannon winced with surprise when Doctor Calvin kneaded a certain spot beneath her breast. "A little. Is that normal?" She tried not to wiggle when the physician came back to touch the same area.

"Tender breast tissue often occurs before one's cycle." Doctor Calvin moved to the other side of the examination table and proceeded to examine her other breast. "How old are you, Shannon?"

"Thirty-seven." Shannon looked at her doctor as she removed her hand from under her paper gown. She watched the woman wash her hands then pick up her chart and write something.

"Hmm. Well, that's a little younger than when I normally schedule my patients to have a mammogram, but I'd like for you to have one." Doctor Calvin lifted her head from the folder in hand.

"A mammogram? Why? Is there something wrong?" Shannon lifted up on her elbows, trying to process the doctor's calm explanation for testing uncharacteristic tissue masses in a woman's breast.

"Look, I can see you're worried and I understand, but try not to freak out over this." Doctor Calvin touched her shoulder. "I just want to be sure there's nothing to be concerned about."

Shannon numbly nodded as the physician started to conduct her annual while reassuring her about the mammogram. Her heart raced as she considered the full implications of what the doctor had said. She barely grimaced from the usual discomfort of the exam Doctor Calvin administered. All she could think about was the lump in her breast and what further testing would reveal.

She left the doctor's office in a bit of a daze with her birth control prescription and appointment for a mammogram scheduled for the following morning. Her cell chimed and she pulled it out of her purse as she entered her limo to see a text message from Jay.

Come with me to Ari's debut performance tonight?

Shannon blew out a breath. She was a little surprised by his invite, given their stilted interactions the previous evening, which had been her fault. Shannon sighed. She knew Jay had been aware something had been up with her but he hadn't pressed the issue. He'd treated her like a gentleman the entire time. She'd decided to try to explain the flurry of emotions swirling within her when they had reached her door but Jay had kissed her softly on the lips and bid her good bye before she'd been able to invite him in. Sadness and need had kept her up most of the night, tossing and turning.

Tears pricked her eyes as she sent back a text accepting Jay's invitation. She really wanted to call and tell him about her doctor's visit but held back. He wasn't her boyfriend. He was just a man she was sleeping with—a respectable, sexy, charming man that enjoyed her company—but she'd be a fool to think it was anything more.

No matter how much she might like for him to be, Jay wasn't the person to share her fears with, and neither was her mother. Never before had she felt so isolated, so alone. "Pathetic." Her whispered voice was drowned out by the wind as she unrolled her window. Shannon didn't bother to wipe away the tear that slid down her cheek as she stared unseeing at the colorful lights passing by.

* * * *

Shannon cursed as she wrenched free the bun she'd been trying to make for the third time. A knock at her door drew another expletive. Her hair was a mess, the dress she'd chosen seemed all wrong and her makeup wasn't done. She should've told Jay she'd meet him at the swanky hotel. Shannon padded barefoot to the door, wishing she had another thirty minutes to get ready.

She pulled open the door, managing a smile despite her internal distress when she saw Jay. He looked and smelled amazing, dressed in dark pants and a yellow button-down shirt that complemented his gorgeous skin tone. "Hello, Jay."

"Hello, yourself." Jay stepped inside her room, his gaze sweeping over her. "You look great."

Shannon dragged her fingers through her wavy, non-blow dried hair. "Oh, please. I look terrible. I'm sorry. I'm not ready. I was going to call you but I forgot. I don't know what happened. Time just got away from me." She gasped when Jay grabbed her and wrapped his arms around her.

"Shh. Take a breath, Red, and *relax*. Ari doesn't sing for another forty-five minutes. We're only twenty minutes away." Jay brushed his lips against her temple. "It's okay, okay?"

Shannon nodded with a little tremor, calmed by his embrace. "Okay."

Jay chuckled. "Good. And when I say you look great, believe me."

"I want to but I don't have on any makeup and this dress..." Shannon tugged at the bodice of it then stilled when Jay kissed her forehead.

"Shannon, look at me."

She lifted her face to his, annoyed by the tears blurring her vision when she saw the tenderness in his gaze.

"Do you really think your makeup or the clothes you wear are what make you beautiful?"

Shannon cleared her throat, trying to dislodge the lump of tears she'd just blinked back. She didn't want to answer his question, didn't like her response.

"It shouldn't take you this long to answer my question, Red."

Shannon pulled away from him. "I think people are drawn to me because of my job, clothing and makeup, yes."

"I'm not asking you what *other* people might think. I'm asking you what *you* think. What makes you beautiful, Shannon? Is it what you wear...? What you do?"

"I don't know." To Shannon's dismay, tears pricked her eyes again, too many to blink back. She prided herself on controlling her emotions most of the time, but Jay's questions, the news from the doctor, her mother's coldness and the mounting need to know if Jay wanted more than just a physical relationship had her feeling more than a little frazzled. Shannon dropped her face from Jay's. "I-I'm sorry, Jay."

"Hey." Jay came back to her side. He lifted her chin, a frown marring his handsome profile when he eyed her tears. "Don't apologize for sharing with me how you feel." Jay cupped her face with both hands. "I'm sorry that you don't know for sure what makes you beautiful. You should." He kissed her lips. "You should absolutely know it and believe it, because it's true. It's not because of what you wear or because of your job either. You're warm, witty, and you genuinely care about others."

"Thanks." Shannon sniffed. "That means a lot."

"I'm not done." Jay released his hold on her face then guided her to stand in front of the full-length mirror in the bedroom. "Look at your face, lovely without any enhancement."

Flattered, Shannon smiled at him through the mirror. "Thank you, Jay."

Jay touched her cheeks. "You're beautiful because of the way you blush when embarrassed or shy." Jay caressed her jaw. "Which to me makes it clear just how big your heart is and that you wear it on your sleeve, although you try to hide that fact. You care about how others feel, which is why you're such an excellent host. I haven't known you long but I've seen you put your feelings aside to please someone else." Jay wrapped his arms around her and nuzzled her neck. "To me, that makes you incredibly beautiful."

"Jay, that's the sweetest thing anyone has ever said to me." Shannon blinked back happy tears this time. "Thank you so much."

"You're welcome." Jay hugged her. "I hope you believe it."

"I do." Shannon turned in his arms to face him, the joy spreading through her making it easy to momentarily forget about everything else. "You focused on personality traits." She reached up and playfully twisted one of his dreads around her finger.

"The most important ones, in my opinion." Jay grinned. "Surprised?"

"A little." She was surprised and delighted. What he'd said meant more to her than any other superficial compliment she'd ever received.

"Hmm. Well, I'd like to discuss the physical traits I find beautiful about you too" — Jay glanced at his watch — "but I don't think we've got enough time for me to talk about every single one right now."

"Why not?"

Jay's smile was electric. "*Because* I plan to kiss them all."

"Mmm. I like the sound of that. I want to play too. There are so many things I find sexy as hell about you as well."

Jay chuckled. "Deal." He lowered his head and claimed her lips in a sensual, panty-wetting kiss that only made her want more.

She sighed when he pulled back. "Oh, please. Can't you kiss and tell me about just *one* physical trait you find beautiful?" Shannon wriggled in his arms, her eyes widening when she brushed against his erection. Desire unfurled within her. Shannon pushed her hand between them to take hold of his cock through his pants, loving Jay's husky groan. "How about I go first?"

Chapter Eight

Jay stood with Shannon to clap for his sister with the rest of the enthusiastic crowd that had gathered to hear her sing. Every candle-lit table in the lounge was occupied. His heart swelled with pride and admiration at the amazing set Ari had just pulled off with her accomplished pianist. Any doubts he'd had about her pursuing a career in music had faded away after her first number. Ari was born to sing — to be on stage — and her performance tonight had proven that.

Tonight had also cemented the fact that he wanted more than just a physical relationship with Shannon. Jay briefly glanced at Shannon as she whistled for his sister. He'd been surprised to find her so out of sorts earlier. He knew not many got to see that side of her and her vulnerability had touched him. Hell, everything about the woman entranced him — her beauty and her heart. She was a remarkable woman and he wanted her to be his.

Jay's gaze dipped to her ruby lips and his cock twitched. Damn, the woman could suck his cock like no other, seemed to crave the taste of him as much as he did her. He'd pulled her up before she'd gotten what she wanted, wanting to come deep inside her instead. Jay discreetly shifted his semi hard-on, aroused by phantom echoes of Shannon's muffled cries of pleasure when he'd taken her up against the wall.

"Your sister is amazing." Shannon turned to him, her green eyes shimmering with excitement. She lifted the exotic bouquet within her grasp. "I hope she likes orchids."

"She'll love those." Jay gave Shannon a reassuring squeeze as he scanned the audience and his gaze locked with Ryder's. He acknowledged the man, more determined than ever to ascertain the exact nature of his sister's connection with him.

"I think I spotted Ryder in the crowd." Shannon squinted in the direction he'd just been looking. "Yep, he's here. Jay, I think my co-host is courting your sister."

"You too? Well, I plan to ask him." Jay glanced back at her sister as she thanked her accompanist. "Ready to give these gorgeous flowers to her?"

Shannon grinned. "Yes." She took hold of his hand as he led the way over to Ari, who smiled broadly when she saw them.

"Hey, you two. I'm so happy you both came." Ari laughed when Shannon presented her with the colorful bouquet. "Aww...these are gorgeous. Thank you, Shannon."

"You're welcome. They match your dress, which is lovely by the way."

"Thanks." Ari smoothed a hand over her crimson cocktail dress. "I must've tried on five dresses before finally deciding on this one." Ari cut her eyes at Jay.

"And there's no need for concern, Jay. I'll pick my next dress to perform in out of my closet."

Jay chuckled. "I didn't say anything."

"Ari, I was in awe of your talent tonight, lady." Shannon placed her hand over her heart. "You were simply *fantastic*."

"Really?" Ari beamed. "I'm so happy to hear you say that."

"It's true." Shannon shook her head. "You interpret songs in a way that makes us experience them in a whole new way. How did it feel being on stage?"

Ari sighed, her gaze dreamy. "Incredible. Jay, what did you think?"

"I think you're a force to be reckoned with behind the mic." Jay grinned when his sister gave him a quick hug with a delighted squeal.

"You're my biggest fan then?"

Jay shot his sister an incredulous look. "Of course. Forever and always, I'll be your number one fan." Jay's gaze narrowed as Ryder approached. "And it would seem I'm not your only admirer."

"What are you talking about?" Ari craned her neck in the direction he was looking then turned back to him with a sheepish smile. "Ryder's cool, so wipe that stern, protective, big brother look off your face."

Shannon laughed. "I enjoy listening to your sibling banter. I always wanted a big brother."

"You have mine." Ari gave Jay and Shannon a cheeky grin. "I mean you *can* have mine."

"Ari." Jay cast a quick glance at Shannon, amused by the pretty blush coloring her cheeks. "One day that smart mouth of yours is going to get you into a heap of trouble."

"Not today, big brother. Not today." Ari giggled as Jay shook his head and Ryder joined them.

"Good evening." Ryder smiled broadly at them. "Erby, you look a little flushed. Are you coming down with something?"

"Thank you for noticing, Ryder." Shannon gave him a wry smirk. "I'm fine."

"Glad to hear it." Ryder shifted his attention to Jay. "Jay, your sister is something else."

"That she is." Jay observed the exchanged looks between his sister and Ryder. "It was nice of you to come out and support her debut performance."

Ryder shrugged. "Wouldn't have missed, especially when she was there for my impromptu debut the other night." Ryder looked at Ari. "Ari, why don't we get your brother and Shannon some champagne to celebrate?"

"Great idea." Ari smiled at Jay and Shannon. "We'll be right back."

"I wonder what's going on with those two." Shannon turned to Jay as his sister and Ryder walked off.

"Me and you both." Jay watched Ari with Ryder. They seemed to be deep in conversation before she stopped to talk to the DJ setting up for the late night crowd. "I just don't get why she always goes for the playboy types."

"They're fun."

Jay shifted his gaze off his sister to look at Shannon. "Fun with no substance?"

"If you realize what you're getting yourself into, fun without substance can have its merits." Shannon scoffed. "Don't look at me that way. Men usually enjoy the latter *way* more than females do."

"*Some* men."

"*Most* men." Shannon shrugged. "I think it's okay for a woman to do so too, if that's what she chooses.

I've dated playboys in the past. I knew exactly what I was getting into and enjoyed those moments for what they were."

"And now?"

Shannon moved closer to him. "Now I'm older and wiser, but sadly playboys are all that seem to hit on me."

"I'm not a playboy, Shannon." Jay stared down at her, holding back the need to crush her against him as her painted lips curved upward.

"I know." Shannon grinned. "You didn't hit on me either, remember?" She leaned in toward him and tapped her finger in time to the R&B song now pumping through the place. "Who kissed who first?"

Jay paused from responding as Ari and Ryder returned with a round of drinks in tow. "Let's toast." Jay took his champagne from Ari and waited for everyone to lift their glasses. "To Ari's successful debut."

"Aww." Ari clinked her glass against everyone's then tasted the bubbly alcohol.

Jay sipped his drink, stepping closer to Ryder as Ari and Shannon started discussing their shoes. "Ryder, I'm just going to get straight to the point—"

"About Ari?" Jay's expression was enigmatic.

"Yep. Hurt her and I'll—"

"I get it, Jay." Ryder grinned. "I respect your lack of subtlety when it matters. Trust me. I'm the same way. I have no intentions of harming Ari."

"Good. She's more fragile than she appears."

Ryder nodded. "I know."

Jay relaxed a little as Ryder switched the conversation back to the show. He decided he'd hold off judgment of the man and actually found himself enjoying Ryder's perspective on certain things on set before his sister and Shannon rejoined them.

"Well"—Ari moved next to Ryder—"earlier, Ryder and I discussed going to dinner and then dancing."

Jay gestured at the couples that were moving to the pulsing beat of the music in the center of the floor. "There's dancing here."

"Not *salsa* dancing. Wanna hook up with us later?"

"No, Ari." Jay chuckled, receiving his sister's code for 'scram' loud and clear. "Shannon and I have other plans."

"Oh, okay then." Ari gave Shannon a quick hug, then Jay. "Have fun, you two."

Jay opened his mouth to return the sentiment then closed it. There was no telling what can of worms his blessing would unleash.

"You guys as well." Shannon gave him a knowing look after they'd all expressed parting good wishes. "You can't hide your uneasiness from me. I know you don't want Ari to have too much fun with Ryder."

"You know what?"

Shannon lifted an expertly shaped eyebrow. "What?"

"I don't want to talk about my sister."

"No?"

"Nope." Jay spanned her waist with his hands and brought her close to his body. "I want to talk about us."

"What about us?" Shannon stared up at Jay, her pulse racing as she followed his dance lead. She drew in a deep breath, mentally preparing herself for his it's-not-you-it's-me speech. He was obviously trying to break up with her and she didn't blame him after her near epic breakdown earlier. Men didn't like conflict. How many times had her mother told her that?

Shannon cursed herself for being so touched by what Jay had said earlier. It had been at that exact moment she'd realized she wanted to mean more to him.

"Shannon, I think you're a wonderful woman. I've enjoyed spending time—"

"Look, just say it, all right?" Shannon faltered in her steps then stood still, blinking to keep the flood of moisture filling her eyes from falling. No way was she going to cry in front of him again. "While I *appreciate* you taking my feelings into consideration by ending things with a gentle touch, I don't need it. I'm a big girl."

"*Ending* things?" Jay tightened his arms around her. "Whoa, Red. You really need to stop jumping to conclusions where I'm concerned. We haven't talked about the nature of our relationship and I wanted to know how you felt. I don't want to *end* what I have with you. I wanted to discuss us because I truly want there to be an *us*. I enjoy being with you, talking and laughing with you, besides the fact that I think you you're the best damn lover I've ever had."

Shannon stared up at him, stunned by his words. "*Oh.*" She relaxed against him, managing a tremulous smile. Her heart pounded in her chest as pure happiness filled her. "Wow. I'm so sorry for interrupting you."

"I'm sorry you thought I wanted to end things between us, especially after today." Jay caressed her cheek with his thumb. "I thought for sure we were on the same page, even though we hadn't talked about it, especially after you opened up emotionally to me in way I'd imagined—or I guessed hoped—you hadn't before with anyone else." Jay loosened his hold on her. "I began to think perhaps you'd want me to be more than just your lover."

"Oh, Jay." Her initial surprise at Jay's words wearing off, Shannon rose up on her tiptoes and kissed him. She wrapped her arms around his neck, letting him take over the kiss, reveling in his strength and the obvious evidence of his desire for her pressed against her thigh.

"So, what do you say, Red? Do you want us to be more?"

"Yes, I do, Jay." Shannon giggled when Jay tightened his hold on her.

"I'm so glad." Jay spun her around in tempo to the rhythmic pulse of the music and Shannon laughed as he brought her back within his arms. "We're good together."

Shannon exhaled against Jay's chest, feeling almost giddy with happiness. Some of her joy faded as she recalled her doctor's appointment the following morning.

"You feel so good in my arms, Red."

Shannon smiled, touched by his words and the way he made her feel. She agreed with him. Being in his arms was the only place she hungered to be. Shannon bit her lip, tormented with the conflicting emotions welling up within her. She wanted to trust her feelings where Jay was concerned, but how could she when she had reservations about sharing her fears about her appointment tomorrow?

Shannon glanced at Jay, the words right on the tip of her tongue, but remained silent. She still felt it was too soon to share something so personal and chances were there was nothing to disclose anyway. Shannon hugged Jay a little tighter, wishing she could tell him how scared she was about her mammogram.

She straightened her posture, taking care to follow Jay's lead as he moved them around the dance floor, her resolve strengthening. She was used to facing life's challenges alone. This one would prove no different.

* * * *

"I'd like to get that tissue biopsied immediately." Doctor Calvin gave her a sympathetic smile. "I can get you into our lab this afternoon if you're free?"

If I'm free? Shannon blinked, trying to grasp all that had been said in the past half hour. *Is this really happening?*

"Shannon?"

Shannon focused on the physician, blinking back tears as she nodded. "This afternoon is fine. I have nowhere to be."

"Great. The sooner I get the test results back, the sooner I can ease your concerns and mine, okay?"

"Okay." Shannon barely heard the rest of what the doctor said before leaving the room. She continued to lie on the examination table after Doctor Calvin left, staring unseeing up at the ceiling.

An unusual mass?

Fear rendered her breathless for a moment. Shannon shook her head as she sat up, inhaling deeply. She couldn't give into her concerns. There simply wasn't time. Taping for the next episode of *Celeb Hotel Chef* was coming up and her mother was arriving tomorrow. She needed to keep it together, at the very least for her career's sake. No matter what, she didn't plan on sharing any of this with her mum. Clarion was incapable of offering any comfort—Shannon knew that without a doubt.

"Be brave." Shannon blinked back tears as she got up off the table. She took a moment to regroup, refusing to delve into what she'd do if the test results showed something abnormal. Despite her numb fingers, somehow she managed to get dressed. She exited the office and made her way down to the lab in a bit of a fog.

* * * *

Shannon was mentally exhausted by the time she finally entered her hotel room the following day. Stripping out of her clothes, she padded into her bathroom. Shannon's gaze was drawn to her chest. Other than a little redness, she was happy the biopsy hadn't left any other detectable mark. Shannon turned on the shower with a deep sigh. Doctor Calvin had ensured her that she'd have the results of her tests tomorrow. Shannon stepped beneath the warm stream of water. She closed her eyes as she worked her favorite soap into a lather all over her skin. This was the first time she'd used her money and her fame to her advantage and it was in order to get a rush on her sample.

Shannon muffled a sob as she exited the shower, wishing there was somebody within her circle she felt comfortable enough to share her feelings with. Her thoughts drifted to Jay as she wrapped a fluffy towel around her. The overwhelming urge to disclose what she was dealing rose up within her again. She walked into the bedroom and glanced at her cell as it chimed then walked over to it. The incoming text message from Jay made her smile, despite her sadness.

Dancing with you the other night was one of the best times I've ever had. Hope you're having a good evening. Mine would be better with you.

Shannon hesitated to reply. She wanted to see him but she didn't know how well she'd be able to hide her scattered emotions. Her hand trembled as she responded.

Feeling tired. Let's get together tomorrow?

Shannon sent the text then sighed when Jay rang her seconds later. "Hello?"

"You all right?"

"I'm fine." Shannon paced the floor. "Why?"

"Because I'm getting this vibe from you that something's bothering you. Is it your mother?"

Shannon scoffed. "No, but she'll be here in less than thirty-six hours to torture me."

"She's attempting to be nice, right?"

Shannon stood still. "My mother can't help being who she is."

"What does that mean?"

"Being 'nice' isn't really part of her nature."

"Red, she loves you. Remember that when she starts to get on your nerves and if need be, call her out on what she says that bothers you."

Shannon squeezed her phone as she briefly closed her eyes. More than anything she just wanted to invite him over.

"Shannon?"

"I'm here. Sorry. I was just thinking about what you were saying. Thanks for the advice, Jay. I appreciate it."

"My pleasure... Speaking of pleasure."

"Come to my room." Shannon sucked in a breath, silently cursing her weakness and her need where Jay was concerned. His husky chuckle made her instantly wet.

"I'll be there in ten minutes."

"Hurry." Shannon grinned as Jay laughed and hung up without another word. She moved over to the suitcase she'd yet to fully unpack and shuffled through its contents, searching for a dusty pink bra and panty set. Her pulse quickened when she located the brand new lingerie. Shannon picked the delicate articles of clothing and went back into the bathroom. She opened her cosmetic tote and took out her makeup. Shannon applied the makeup to the reddened area on the side of her breast, blending the powder into her skin until she was satisfied with the results. With any luck, Jay would be too distracted to notice anything out of the ordinary.

Shannon smiled as she put on her lingerie. She pivoted to see her body from all angles. The color of the fabric against her skin was sublime. Shannon released her ginger tresses from the loose knot fixed upon her head, shaking the unruly waves loose unto her shoulders. She couldn't wait for Jay to see her. Her lips curved upward when she heard knocking. Shannon hurried from the bedroom without bothering to put on a robe. She opened the door slightly, taking care not to reveal her state of undress. "Good evening, Jay."

"It is now." Jay grinned. "Are you going to let me in, Red?"

Shannon stayed behind the door as she moved back to let Jay pass. She pushed the door closed, pivoting with a giggle when he swore. "Do you like?" Shannon sashayed toward him, enjoying his frank appraisal.

She drank in the sight of him, so striking in his dark jeans and slate gray Henley shirt. He'd pulled back his dreads, and Shannon's gaze was drawn to his handsome profile. Her heart thudded with anticipation when he reached out to touch her hair.

"You know I do." Jay shook his head as his gaze drifted over her. "You are *so* pretty in pink."

"Thank you."

"You're welcome." Jay dropped his hand to her breast, and Shannon trembled as he teased her nipple through the bra. He slid his other hand over her hip and into her panties to cup her ass cheek. "It's almost a crying shame that I plan to strip you out of these."

Shannon pressed her body against his, comforted by his warmth and strength. Being with him tonight was definitely better than spending it alone worrying about tomorrow. She smiled when his choice of words sparked a thought. "I've got a better idea."

"One better than you naked?"

Shannon stepped back from him, laughing as he groaned. "You'll see. Why don't you have a seat in that chair?"

Jay lifted an eyebrow but followed her instruction as she padded over to the stereo. She turned it on before she could lose her nerve and hit play on the Prince CD she had been listening to earlier. Shannon kept her back to Jay, closed her eyes and wriggled her hips to the pulsing beat of *Kiss*. Jay's soft curse behind her spurred her on. Shannon unclasped her bra, shucked it to the floor and spun around with her hands covering her breasts.

Any lingering nerves disappeared when saw the smoldering look of desire in Jay's eyes. She lowered her hands, revealing her hard nipples to Jay as she pushed her panties down. Shannon gyrated closer to him then laughed when he grabbed her and pulled her down onto his lap. Breathless, she wiggled against his hard-on. "Hey! I wasn't done."

Jay gave her a wicked grin. "Good, because I want a lap dance."

Shannon unbuttoned and unzipped his pants, shivering with need as he kissed the side of her breast then licked the tip. "I don't know if I've got the right moves." She shifted her position to straddle him.

"I'll keep you on beat." Jay extracted a foil packet from his pocket and ripped open the package.

The edge in his voice made her smile as she released his cock from his underwear and helped him roll the condom on. Shannon raised up, positioned the head of his dick to her slick entrance and they both groaned as she slowly took him in. She winced despite her wetness as her body stretched to accommodate him before moaning when she was fully seated. Shannon placed her hands behind her on Jay's hard thighs and began to rock on him, gingerly at first then faster as the sensations of pleasure sharpened.

Jay slipped his hand beneath her, increasing the pace and Shannon gasped. She brought one hand between her legs to caress her clit, widening the arc of ecstasy within her that was threatening to snap. Her mewling and the roar of her heartbeat thundering in her ears drowned out the seductive song playing as she climaxed. She clung to Jay, overwhelmed by every blissful wave of her orgasm, and he kept his word by keeping her on beat until he found his own release.

Chapter Nine

"Damn." Jay scowled backstage as Ryder announced to the world that Kelly had lost the cook-off challenge to Oscar. He had been rooting for the spunky chef the entire time but when she'd scorched her white sauce, he'd had known her chances of winning had been slim to none.

Jay eyed Shannon as she held the mic in front of Kelly, giving her an opportunity to speak. Shannon looked amazing, the elegant cut of her strapless black dress highlighting her slender body and long legs. Jay liked it when she wore her hair down. Tonight, the vibrant tresses fell in soft waves around her bare shoulders. Once again they'd lacked sufficient time to talk before the show, but Jay had sensed that Shannon had still been out of sorts and he wanted to know why.

Last night with Shannon had been imprinted on his brain. He'd left her reluctantly the next morning, hoping they'd spend the day together but Shannon had claimed she'd needed time to prepare for her mother's arrival tomorrow. Understandable, but Jay realized he was selfish when it came to Shannon. He needed *his* time with her and he was looking forward to their dinner plans after the show.

Applause on the set focused his attention back on Kelly as she exited the stage. He took a step forward as she approached. "Kelly, I'm so sorry."

"Me too. He's a cocky bastard. I hope you beat him, Jay." Kelly gave him a quick hug, her eyes shimmering with tears when she pulled away. "Thank you for being such a cool guy."

"Kelly, you're an amazing chef. I know you'll go far in your future endeavors."

Kelly nodded. "Thanks, Jay." She offered him a wobbly smile. "I'm going to be mad at you if you don't beat him."

"I'll be mad too. Don't worry, I'm going to do my best to whip his ass next round." Jay grinned as she laughed.

"Well, it won't be easy. You guys have to make prepare two dishes for the final competition."

Jay shrugged. "I'm not worried. I might even do that victory dance for you if I do win."

"You mean *when* you win."

Jay chuckled. "That's right, *when*."

"I'll say goodbye before I head back home." Kelly straightened her back. "All is not lost, I suppose. I think I've made a possible love connection."

"Vicki?"

Kelly nodded, some of the sadness leaving her eyes. "Yep. She's made me promise to teach her how to cook."

Jay grinned, thinking of his own cooking lessons with Shannon. "The right cooking lesson can be the ultimate aphrodisiac."

"I know, right?" Kelly sighed. "God, I wish I didn't have to wait here for the show to end. If it weren't for the fact I think Oscar would blab to the media that I ran off with my tail between my legs, I'd leave already."

"I'll stand beside you. No worries." Jay waited for the cheers to die down as Shannon and Ryder bid the audience good night. "I plan on winning, Kelly, for your sake and mine."

Kelly grinned and mouthed "Thank you" to him as Ryder, Shannon and Oscar approached. "Congratulations, Oscar."

"How gracious of you. Thanks." Oscar shifted his attention to Jay when Kelly didn't rush to respond to his condescending tone. "Well, I guess it's just you and me now, Dax." Oscar offered a wide smile that didn't quite reach his eyes.

"Indeed it is." Jay kept his gaze on Oscar while being completely aware of Shannon talking to Ryder to his left. "I'm up to the challenge. Are you?"

"We'll see." Oscar chuckled. "I've gotta say I'm feeling pretty confident. Desserts are my forte."

"Sweet." Jay held back saying more. There was no need to. Come tomorrow night, he'd bring his A-game and show Oscar Blithe once and for all that talk was cheap, regardless of the recipe.

"Well, I'm off to party before I pack." Kelly unbuttoned the collar of her uniform. "I'll be watching to see Jay win." She flicked Oscar a frosty smile then walked off.

"You know, I'm almost sad to see her go." Oscar scratched his chin as she stared after her. "She was entertaining, if nothing else." He smiled at a pretty brunette production assistant passing by them.

Jay snorted. "*You're* entertaining, if nothing else, too."

"See, I feel that way about you too. I guess we do have something other than cooking in common. Later, Dax." Oscar chuckled then headed off in the direction of the woman he'd just been eyeing.

"Jerk." Jay hoped no one overheard him as he headed over to Shannon and Ryder.

"Congrats, man." Ryder shook his hand.

"Thanks, Ryder." Jay glanced at Shannon, more than tempted to reach out and twist one of her red locks around his finger. "Were you two surprised with the results of the cook-off challenge?"

Shannon leaned in toward both men. "More like disappointed." She smiled when they both laughed.

Ryder turned to Jay. "Is Ari here?"

"No. She texted and told me she wouldn't be able to get here in time."

"Hmm." Ryder glanced at his phone. "I thought she was meeting me here."

"Did you two go out last night?" Shannon asked the question Jay had been curious to know the answer to.

Ryder grinned. "We did. I think I might play for her set next week. The lounge manager loved the vibe the two of us had on stage."

"Ari seems to really like this gig. I hope her enthusiasm continues." Jay looked around, searching for sight of her. "She tends to lose interest in things—*men*—quickly. No offense, Ryder."

"Some taken." Ryder chuckled as Jay and Shannon laughed. "Ari was born to sing. I can't imagine her losing interest in this job anytime soon."

"Hope you're right. The best part of her working is that it limits her time in the casinos. Thank God the novelty of gambling here has finally seemed to wear off." Jay thought he saw Ryder's smile slip. "Has she been gambling with you?"

"Not with me." Ryder lifted his phone with an apologetic look. "I've gotta take this call. I'll talk to you two later."

"Bye." Shannon turned to Jay as he walked off. "Ryder can be obnoxious but he's not a bad guy."

"I didn't say he was."

Shannon exhaled. "I know. Just trying to reassure."

"You're sweet, and stunning in that dress." Jay glanced around them. "I want to kiss you right now."

Shannon smiled. "So kiss me."

"Here in front of everyone?"

She nodded, uncaring of an audience. After the morning she'd had, his kiss was what she needed more than anything. "Right here. Right now."

The air charged around them as Jay put his arm around her waist, brought her in close and claimed her lips. Shannon welcomed his kiss, wrapped her arms around his neck, heedless of the appreciative whistles going on around them. Shannon melted into him, feeling more at ease within his embrace than she had all day.

"Shannon?"

Her mother's incredulous voice penetrated through her blissful fog. Shannon wrenched her face from Jay's, her eyes widening when she saw Clarion. "*Mum*, what are you doing here?" She felt Jay's arm tighten around her supportively when she stiffened against him. "I thought you were coming tomorrow." Shannon pulled away from Jay to give her mother a quick hug and she was enveloped with the familiar scent of her mum's favorite perfume.

"Well…" Clarion straightened the lacy teal shawl around her tanned shoulders, her gold bangles jingling as she smoothed her perfectly coifed hair. She looked none the worse for wear after her flight, dressed in the fashionable white sheath dress and teal sandals. Clarion's gaze narrowed as she stared at them. "I decided to come a day early and surprise you but I guess *I'm* the one who's surprised."

Shannon forced a chuckle. She cast a quick glance a Jay, knowing exactly what 'surprise' her mother was referring to. "Mum, this is Jay Dax. Jay, my mother Clarion Erby."

"It's a pleasure to meet you, Mrs. Erby." Jay offered his hand and Clarion shook it. "I now see where Shannon gets her beauty."

Clarion gave Jay her practiced smile. "Why, thank you. And please, call me Clarion." Clarion turned to Shannon. "I already checked into my room. It's lovely. I'll definitely stay at a Banner Hotel again. Have you eaten? Because I'm starved."

"I haven't. Jay and I were just discussing where we were going to grab a bite."

"You two should go ahead." Jay placed his hand on the small of Shannon's back and she leaned into it, wishing more than anything for his undivided attention. "As executive chef for Banner Hotel restaurant, I would recommend eating there for your first night in Vegas."

Clarion raised an eyebrow. "Oh?"

"Absolutely." Jay grinned. "The food and ambience is amazing. I do think you'd enjoy."

"Would you personally guarantee I would?"

Shannon sighed at her mother's snooty challenge.

"I would personally see that you did." Jay subtly increased his hold on Shannon as he chuckled, seemingly unfazed by Clarion's challenge.

"Excellent." Clarion looked at Shannon. "Can you leave now?"

"I need a few minutes to gather my things."

Clarion nodded. "Fine. I'll return some phone calls and wait for you here."

"Okay." Shannon attempted to ignore the slivers of guilt coursing through her for wanting to spend the evening with Jay and not her mother.

Clarion shifted her gaze to Jay. "It was nice to meet you, Jay."

"And you, Clarion. I can't wait to hear your feedback about tonight's dining experience."

"Are you going to prepare our meal?"

Shannon held back a sigh, embarrassed by her mum's assumption everyone should cater to her needs. She glanced at Jay to see if he was offended by Clarion's question but he only flashed her mom his signature smile.

"It would be my pleasure to. You ladies decide on the time and I'll make sure I'm there."

Clarion nodded. "Wonderful."

"I'll be right back, Mum." Shannon tried to push back feelings of anxiety as she walked off with Jay. She had wanted the extra time to mentally prepare for her mother's visit. It was just like Clarion to change her plans without regard to how it affected Shannon's.

"Jay, you don't have to go into work tonight for my mum," Shannon said once they were out of earshot. She opened the door to her dressing room and stepped inside, aware of Jay closing it behind them.

"She's a firecracker." Jay chuckled. "I'm surprised she's not a redhead."

"Oh, she is." Shannon removed the dangly gemstone earrings her stylist had picked out for her. "She's been blonde for so long, I forget. She always wanted me to dye my hair too."

"What?" Jay came over to her. He lifted one of her locks. "No way. I can't imagine it any other shade."

Shannon smiled. "I know. I'll never forget you showing me why you considered it one of my most beautiful physical traits." She giggled as Jay took her into his arms, remembering how he compared the hue of her tresses to her areolas. He'd circled them over and over with her hair. "You've got a *real* thing for redheads."

"Just one." Jay palmed her ass. "Is your mom going to have a problem with us?"

"She has a problem with everything." Shannon shrugged. "I don't care what she thinks about us. She's never had a clue as to the type of man I would want. I'll have to deal with her disappointment that Ryder will not be her son-in-law."

"Ryder?"

"Mmm...hmm." Shannon laughed when Jay growled. "That's almost the exact same noise I made when she tried for the umpteenth time to play matchmaker. Seriously, I'll take her somewhere else to eat."

Jay playfully squeezed her bottom. "You will not. I don't mind cooking something special for you both."

"You're amazing. You know that? I-I...never expected that crazy kiss we shared months ago to lead to this." Shannon trembled against him as he pressed his lips to her temple. Her heart skipped a beat at how close she'd been to uttering those three crazy, irrational words.

"I know." Jay kissed her then groaned. "Tell me to let you go."

"Don't want to." Shannon rested her head on his chest.

"Okay, but if you don't, I'll be further tempted to take you in here again."

Shannon gasped as she lifted her face to his. "Not with my mother here! She probably got impatient waiting, decided to come find me and is standing right outside my door by now."

"Then you'd better say it." Jay shrugged, the glint in his eyes full of mirth. "I'm getting harder by the second, Red." He shifted in a way to prove his point.

"Let me go." Shannon wriggled in his arms, laughing as he released her.

"I hope you enjoy your mom's visit."

"You and me both." Shannon walked with him to the door. "I'll call you later." She gave him a quick kiss then opened the door to see her mother standing only a few feet away.

"Okay." Jay stepped into the hallway, waved to Clarion then turned back to Shannon with a wry chuckle. "You were right."

Shannon sighed. "Unfortunately."

"Thank goodness you said those magic words." Jay grinned as he pivoted.

Shannon watched him walk in the opposite direction of her mother, who headed toward her. "I need a few minutes to change."

"I thought that's what you were doing." Clarion peeked inside her dressing room. "Aren't you going to invite me, or do you only allow totally unsuitable bachelors?"

Shannon stepped back to let her mother in, feeling a whoosh of heat surge up within her as she fought back the urge to yell. She closed her door with a little more effort than was necessary then whirled around. "And why would you say Jay is 'totally unsuitable', Mother?"

Clarion sighed. "Come on, Shannon. Do I really need to spell that out for you?"

"Yes, you really do." Shannon unzipped the side of her dress and shimmed out of it. She donned a pair of pink capris and a bohemian styled floral shirt to match.

"I mean, he seems like a nice man, but a *cook?*" Clarion waved a hand. "My daughter can do better. I had the pleasure of being introduced to Ryder. What a charming man. So handsome too."

"Ryder is a nice guy." Shannon struggled to keep her voice even, angered by her mum's dismissive comments about Jay. She sat down at her vanity to check her makeup. "I've enjoyed working with him."

"See?" Clarion smiled. "I knew you two would have chemistry. You've got so much in common. He's in show business. He's single, rich and—"

"White?" Shannon tossed her locks over her shoulders as she spritzed a little hairspray to maintain her loose waves. She leveled her gaze with her mother's in the mirror.

"Shannon!"

"What? Isn't that one of the unspoken criteria for any man I'm to date or marry?" Shannon slipped her feet into a pair of white sandals as her mum stared at her.

"I've never said that to you." Clarion seemed to pale beneath her tan.

"Not verbally, no. You subtly mentioned that I could do better, casting Jay unworthy because of his job, which is ridiculous. Jay Dax is not just a 'cook'. He's one of the *best* chefs in the country. He's an executive chef for one of the finest hotels around." Shannon buckled her sandals. "And FYI... I am dating him and I will *not* discuss *your* feelings about *my* relationship any further." She ignored her mother's shocked expression, offering a polite smile as she stood and faced her. "I want to enjoy our time together here in Vegas. Don't you?"

Clarion gasped. "What's gotten into you lately?"

Shannon thought about the test she'd taken earlier that week and the niggling fears she'd been trying to ignore all day. "I just don't want to argue. Our time together is short. You said you were hungry. Do you want to go grab a drink or a small bite before dinner?"

"No." Clarion huffed, clearly at a rare loss of words after Shannon's torrent of them. "You know I don't like eating in between meals."

Shannon went over to her and pressed a kiss on her cheek, wanting to ease the tension between them. "I do know. So, what do you want to do? This is your first time in Sin City. I want it to be a memorable one."

Her mum gave her a small smile. "I'd love to do some sightseeing."

"Okay." Shannon stuffed her phone into her purse. "I'm ready. We can go. How was your flight in?" She walked to the door and opened it, half-listening to her mum's response. Her mind was on what the doctor would have to say and what she'd almost said to Jay. Shannon made a concentrated effort to listen to her mum, determined to pull it together and show her a good time. She'd have to wait to deal with her scattered emotions later.

Chapter Ten

Jay added a slice of lime as garnish to the second round of mango margaritas he'd personally prepared for Shannon and Clarion.

"Damn, this lady's got you mixing drinks?" Bret grinned as Jay placed napkins on the tray he held. "You've never done that before."

"You're pretty busy." Jay gestured around the packed bar counter. "I just thought I'd ease your burden by two drinks."

"Uh huh." Bret shook his head with obvious amusement as he walked off.

Jay headed over to Shannon's table. He caught sight of her laughing and smiled, pleased dinner with her mom appeared to be going well. "Here you are, ladies."

"Yum, Jay, thank you." Shannon took her glass from him. "Everything was so good."

Clarion nodded, taking a sip of her drink. "It certainly was. I want that filet mignon recipe."

"I'm afraid I can't give away my trade secrets." Jay chuckled when Clarion pouted.

"Well, I guess I can understand that." Clarion sat back in her seat as a server removed their remaining dishes. "Do you offer cooking lessons?"

Shannon coughed and Jay grinned as their gazes met, knowing she was picturing their erotic cooking sessions the same way he was, if the color flooding her cheeks was any indication. "Working here doesn't leave me much time to offer those. I'm so glad dining here tonight has been a good experience for you, Clarion."

"Can't you join us for a moment, Jay?"

"Sure."

Clarion's invitation must have surprised Shannon more than Jay. Her green eyes sparkled with happiness as he took his seat next to Shannon. "Do you two have any room for dessert? I didn't make the dark chocolate brownie with macaroons and raspberry sauce, but I can vouch for the fact that they are out of this world."

"Oh, I shouldn't." Clarion placed her hand on her trim waistline, her tone wistful.

"You absolutely should." Jay glanced at Shannon when she touched his thigh under the table. "This is Sin City. You should indulge a little." His cock immediately responded to her tiny squeeze on his leg.

"He's right, Mum. I'll share it with you."

Clarion frowned. "I hope you aren't indulging too often, Shannon. You know that television —"

"Adds ten pounds," Shannon finished, the light in her eyes dimming. "Yes, I know."

Jay covered his hand over Shannon's when she started to remove it from his leg. "Shannon could gain twenty pounds and television viewers would be none the wiser."

Shannon gave him a grateful smile and Jay couldn't resist leaning over to kiss her cheek. He reined in the need to pull her hair free from the bun she'd fashioned, glad to see some of the sparkle back in her gaze as she intertwined her fingers with his.

Clarion cleared her throat, clearly uncomfortable. "I think I'll just have a coffee."

"I'll have that order put in for you." Jay shifted his attention back to Shannon. "I'm going to pop in on Ari's set tonight. You both are welcome to come."

"Okay." Shannon pulled her fingers free of his to press her hand to his semi-erect cock. "That feels...*sounds* good."

Jay held back a chuckle as Clarion frowned and Shannon surreptitiously snatched her hand away. He stood, grateful for the length of his chef uniform. "Shall I have a coffee brought over for you too?"

"Yes." Shannon cast a glance at her mother then looked at Jay. "Dessert another time."

"All right. Two espressos coming up. Good night, Clarion. Shannon, we'll talk later." Jay smiled as Shannon nodded and they both bid him goodnight. He walked off, knowing there would definitely be dessert later. Jay greeted members of his staff as he weaved his way through the crowded restaurant to the kitchen. Satisfied things were flowing smoothly, Jay informed his crew he was leaving. He headed to his office in the back, changed out of his uniform and checked his voicemail before leaving.

Less than thirty minutes later, Jay entered the venue where his sister performed. The place was already packed. The soft jazz ballads playing could barely be heard over the patrons laughing and talking. Jay scanned the room but didn't catch sight of Ari. He glanced at his watch then frowned. Her band wasn't on stage setting up, which was strange considering she was supposed to be singing in less than ten minutes.

"Jay."

Jay turned to see Ryder. "Hey, what's up? Have you seen Ari?"

"Fuck." Ryder dragged a hand through hair, his expression grave. "Man, I think your sister is in trouble."

"What?" Jay took a step closer to Ryder, his heart twisting with worry as the man shook his head. Ari really was going to be the death of him. "What the hell is going?"

"I wasn't going to say anything but—"

Jay took hold of Ryder's shirt. "Tell me what's going on now."

"I will"—Ryder glanced at Jay's clenched fist, his gaze stony—"but *you're* going to have to take your damn hands off me right now."

"Hey, you two."

Both men turned their heads to see Ari. She placed her hand on Jay's arm, all breathless giggles and smiles. "What's going on here?"

Jay released Ryder to scowl at his sister. "You tell me, Ari. Ryder says you're in some kinda trouble?"

Ari's grin slipped a little. "Trouble? Uh...well, I'm running late and my accompanist bailed last minute. Ryder was concerned I wouldn't make it here in time to perform, but here I am!" Ari put her other hand on Ryder. "Can you please accompany me? You know the songs."

Jay looked at Ryder, sensing something unspoken being said between the two as Ryder slowly nodded. "Are you sure that's all that is going on?"

"*Yes.* Now I have to scoot. My set starts in two minutes." Ari pressed a kiss on Jay's cheek then tugged on Ryder. "We need to get up there."

"Okay." Ryder shifted his gaze to Jay, his expression now unreadable. "Are you going to stay and listen?"

"I'm not going anywhere." Jay glanced at Ari who exhaled, no doubt knowing from the look on his face that their conversation was far from over.

"Sweet." Ari smoothed a hand over her short, lime-green dress. "We'll talk after. Wish us luck?"

"You got it." Jay tilted his head in Ryder's direction then watched the two walked off, still suspicious as hell as to what was really going on. He sought out a seat, determined to get the answers he wanted from Ari later. There was no way Ryder had come up to him the way he had just to update him on Ari's tardiness. Something else was up and he had every intention of finding out what it was.

* * * *

Shannon peeked at her watch and sighed, wondering what was taking the doctor so long to come in. She had a lunch date with her mum in a half hour and Clarion would be annoyed if she had to wait more than five minutes for her. Shannon glanced at the plastic model of a woman's reproductive system sitting on top of the counter across from her. She suppressed a shudder, unnerved by the waiting and the nagging feeling something was wrong. A soft knock on the door drew her attention off the female replica to Dr. Calvin as she stepped inside.

"Hello, Shannon." She gave Shannon a gentle smile. "How are you?" Dr. Calvin rolled over a chair then took a seat in front of Shannon.

"I'll be much better after you share the results of my biopsy." Shannon clasped her hands together to keep from fidgeting.

Dr. Calvin nodded. "I know these past few days must have been stressful and I wish I didn't have to add to it with my news. Shannon, you have what is called an invasive ductal carcinoma. I'd like to run some other tests to find out exactly what we're dealing with but—"

"W-Wait." Shannon struggled to say the words swirling around in the wind tunnel roaring in her head. "Are you saying I have *cancer*? Breast cancer?"

"Yes, but we've caught it early and this is typically a less aggressive type." Dr. Calvin touched her hand. "I'm confident we will eradicate this disease from your body."

Shannon gasped as she shook her head, tears blurring her vision. "Oh my God. This isn't happening." Her hand shook as she accepted the tissues offered to her by the doctor and attempted to dry her damp cheeks. The words *cancer* and *disease*, seemed to echo within the small space. She'd just come in for contraceptives. Now she had cancer? It didn't make sense, couldn't be true.

"Shannon, I know it's scary to hear this diagnosis but as I said, I'm hopeful that we can get rid of the cancer and get you healthy in no time. Okay?"

Shannon numbly nodded, half-listening to the doctor explain the type of cancer she had and the treatment options available. Her mind was blown. She couldn't focus on anything other than holding back the scream burning the back of her throat.

"Shannon?"

Shannon blinked and slowly lifted her head to meet the doctor's concerned gaze. "W-What?"

"I don't think you heard my question. How long will you be working here in Vegas?"

Shannon shrugged. "A few more weeks? It depends on how this show goes...whether there will be another one."

"I understand. Well, I will be able to make my recommendation on how fast we need to move forward with your treatment after I get your other tests back. You may very well be able to put things off until you're back home." Dr. Calvin wrote something in Shannon's medical file then looked at her. "Do you have any questions for me?"

Shannon stared at the woman. She tried to swallow down the hysterical giggle fit surging up within her. There were a million questions she wanted to ask but there was just one that she wanted an answer to right now. "Am I going to die?"

"Oh, Shannon." Doctor Calvin's gaze softened. "I don't believe so. I believe we are going to work together to kick cancer's ass and win. A positive attitude—having hope—can make all the difference in the world. All right?"

Shannon nodded again, not trusting herself to speak. She had no idea how she was going to get through lunch with her mother or the taping happening in several hours.

"Deidre at the front desk will help you set up an appointment with the lab. Take as long as you need in here. Is there someone out in the waiting room you'd like for me to send for to be back here with you?"

Shannon shook her head. "I came alone. It's okay."

"All right." Dr. Calvin gave her another sympathetic look. "I'll be in touch."

Shannon thanked the physician and watched her leave through a haze of fresh tears. She got off the examination table on shaky legs and went over to her purse. Shannon took out her compact, opened it and stared at her blotchy, tear-streaked face. Dismayed, Shannon reached into her bag for her makeup. She needed to pull it together before meeting up with her mum. Getting her diagnosis *and* telling her mother about it was not something she could deal with all in the same day.

There was only one person she wanted to share her terrible news with.

Jay.

Shannon let out a sob then straightened her spine. She wasn't ready to tell him yet either. Doing so would truly test whether or not they had more than a fling going and she didn't think she could handle any more heart-breaking revelations.

* * * *

Jay clasped his hands behind his back as he walked to his station, satisfied with the presentation of his dishes before the judges. His gaze drifted to Shannon. Damn, he'd missed being with her last night. He had been half tempted to call her more than once, despite knowing she was showing her mom a good time for her last night in Vegas.

"In just a short while we will know who will become our first Celeb Hotel Chef." The audience applauded as Shannon nodded. Her beauty and poise never ceased to mesmerize him. Tonight she wore a shimmering gray gown that accentuated her svelte body. It went all the way to the floor but the slit on the side offered tempting glimpses of her legs and her ridiculously high silver stilettos. "Chef Dax and Chef Blithe have created two very different entrees and desserts for the judges tonight. Whose will win, based on presentation, taste and use of tonight's secret ingredient?"

"I don't know, Shannon"—Ryder moved to stand next to Shannon between Jay and Oscar's stations—"but I can't wait to find out."

Jay glanced at Oscar, met his I-know-I've-whipped-your-ass gaze and grinned. God, he hoped he'd done enough to wipe that cocky smirk off the chef's face. It would be interesting to see. Blood oranges had been revealed as the secret ingredient for their courses. They had both selected the salmon fillets to work with for their entrée but had taken different directions for their desserts.

"Jay, how does it feel to have finished tonight's double challenge?" Ryder gave him a practiced smile and Jay returned it. The two of them had yet to discuss whatever had been going on with Ari the other night.

"It feels great. I'm pleased with my work and I think the judges will appreciate the depth of flavors in my dishes."

Ryder nodded. "Did you think the fight for the *Celeb Hotel Chef* title would come down between you and Oscar?"

"Oscar has been a formidable opponent from the start." Jay looked at Oscar. "We've both worked hard tonight. I can't wait to find out what the judges think."

"Chef Blithe, did you think you'd be standing here as one of the final two tonight?"

"Of course." Oscar smiled. "I'll be surprised if I'm not the *last* chef standing up here." Oscar waved a pair of tongs in response to the lively crowd's cheers and boos.

Shannon shook her head, a good natured grin curving her glossy lips. "Tell us what you've prepared for our judges."

"Sure." Oscar set the tongs down. "I pan-seared the king salmon then prepared a blood orange vinaigrette for it. The vinaigrette is infused with white wine vinegar, olive oil, butter, fresh cracked white pepper and fresh chives top it off. The creamy garlic risotto is the perfect side to complement the savory flavors of the fish. I also incorporated the secret ingredient in my flaky blood orange tart, drizzled with a deep, dark salted butter caramel sauce. This sweet treat is a sinful combination of texture and flavors. This rustic crostata tastes as wonderful as it looks."

"Sounds delicious, doesn't it?" Shannon smiled at the applauding audience.

"Sure does, Shannon." Ryder directed his mic to Jay. "Chef Dax, what did you make to top that?"

"The judges tasted my glazed salmon topped with blood orange salsa. This glaze really adds depth to the fish with fresh ginger, red chili flakes, stone ground mustard all infused with the juice of the blood oranges." Jay grinned at the audience as they oohed and ahhed. "I then topped the seafood with my salsa made out of the fruit with scallions, ginger, chili peppers and crushed cumin seeds, a little bit of salt and pepper and fresh cilantro. I paired the main dish with a simple house salad dressed with a blood orange inspired vinaigrette. For dessert, I whipped together a blood orange flan with blood orange caramel." Jay nodded as the crowd applauded. "I just love how the lightness of the custard is highlighted by the sweetness of the caramel and the juicy tartness of the fruit. Lemon zest and vanilla beans set off all of the flavors to absolute perfection."

"Mmm. Very nice. I wouldn't have thought to pair salsa and seafood. Is it a tasty collaboration or a food fusion gone wrong? We're about to find out from our esteemed panel of judges." Ryder walked with Shannon over to the judges table.

"Yes, we are. Judges, what's the verdict?"

Jay briefly met Shannon's gaze as she asked the question to the panel and determined he didn't care if he lost, as long as she was his woman.

"Wow, was this a tough decision for us." Don Mackey licked his lips. "Both of the dishes we sampled were delicious. Chef Blithe's vinaigrette popped with flavor and really brought out the taste of the fish. His risotto was perfectly cooked, the quintessential complement to his main entrée and his buttery tart was divine. Chef Dax's salmon was a surprising blend of savory and sweet. The salsa truly brought out the flavor of the fish and his salad had just the right amount of tart sweetness to set the entire meal off to absolute perfection. A true flan connoisseur, I admired Chef Dax's mastery of the blood oranges with this decadent, creamy dessert. I will asking him for his recipe." Don Mackey rested his clasped hands on his rounded belly.

Ryder chuckled. "Well, don't keep us in suspense any longer. Who is the winner?"

"It was not an easy decision, Ryder." Bernard briefly glanced at the other judges, his smile wide. "Both chefs should be proud of what they accomplished here this evening. Chef Dax showcased and used the secret ingredient in every aspect of his meal." Bernard sat forward in his chair. "In the end, our decision was unanimous. Chef Dax is our Celeb Hotel Chef!"

Jay grinned, delighted by the roar of the audience's approval and their final decision. He waved to the crowd as Shannon and Ryder clapped. Jay walked over to Oscar with his hand outstretched.

"Congratulations, Jay." Oscar tilted his head in Jay's direction.

"Thanks, Oscar. It was a pleasure whipping your ass."

Oscar chuckled. "I deserved that. Do me a favor and get the hell outta my face? It's really hard to maintain this stupid ass smile for the cameras."

Jay laughed and obliged, moving back to his station as Shannon and Ryder came over to present him with the golden knife.

Ryder beckoned to him. "Chef Dax, please join us in front here."

Jay walked to stand in between both hosts, raising his hand again to acknowledge the applauding audience.

"Chef Dax, congratulations. You *are* our first Celeb Hotel Chef." Ryder handed him the trophy with one hand and offered his other.

Jay shook his hand as he took the prize. "Thank you, Ryder." He turned to Shannon and the look of pride and happiness glimmering in her green eyes twisted something in his heart.

"Congratulations, Chef Dax." Shannon gave him a hug and Jay wrapped one arm around her.

"Thank you, Shannon." Jay felt her tremble against him and frowned when she sagged a little against him as the crowd went wild. He tightened his hold on her to keep her upright, noticing how pale she was beneath the bright lights. Jay frowned as he steadied her. Knowing she wouldn't want to appear ill on live television, Jay tried to surreptitiously brace her body against his. Something was wrong with Shannon. Jay's heart pounded in his chest as the realization hit him like a ton of bricks. Time seemed to stand still but in reality no more than a few seconds could have passed as Shannon sucked in a breath and moved away from him.

"You're welcome."

Jay was amazed her voice didn't warble as she walked away from him. His win forgotten, Jay tuned out her and Ryder's closing remarks, his attention focused on Shannon. *What the hell just happened?*

Chapter Eleven

Shannon waved to her mother before she disappeared into the corridor leading to the plane. She breathed a sigh of relief as she pivoted and walked toward her exit. Her feet ached in her heels but Shannon didn't slow her pace as she slipped her designer shades on. The last twelve hours had been hell, pretending to have a good time, to be okay. There hadn't been a moment to stop and catch her breath, what with the end of the show party being right after the taping.

At least Clarion had enjoyed the celebration. Shannon didn't know whether to be relieved or upset her mother had been none the wiser that she was upset. Jay had questioned her about her strange episode during the show but she'd managed to deflect his queries. She still couldn't believe that it had happened. If Jay hadn't been standing beside her... Jay had subtly saved her from a possible PR nightmare and he knew it. Thankfully, with all the photo ops and commotion, there hadn't been a real opportunity for them to talk further.

Shannon took her vibrating cell out of her purse and saw a text message from Jay to confirm their plans later. She'd missed him last night, couldn't wait to be alone with him—to be in his arms.

The heat of the day still simmered in the night wind washing over Shannon as she pushed through the glass doors leading outside. She acknowledged her driver as he opened the door to her limo. Shannon slid into her seat and exhaled again, grateful her visit with her mother was over, despite how well it had gone.

Exhaustion made her lean back in the leather seat and close her eyes. She needed a warm shower, a change of clothes and Jay. He deserved something special for the way he'd covered for her on national television. She'd been on the verge of fainting and his touch, his strength, had been the only things that had helped her center her being. It had taken all of her acting skills to convince him at the after party that she'd just been tired, that there was nothing seriously wrong and no she didn't need to see a doctor. Shannon sighed at the cruel truth.

"Ms. Erby? We're here."

Shannon opened her eyes, startled by the sound of her driver's voice. She hadn't realized she'd fallen asleep. "Thanks, Clyde." Shannon waited for him to get out and open her door, giving him a warm smile as she exited. She entered the back of hotel, moving toward the private elevator on autopilot.

Less than twenty minutes later, she stepped beneath the warm stream of water in her shower. She lathered her hair then her body. Her fingers moved over her breasts and she caressed them, weighing them in her hands. She tested their sensitivity by plucking at her nipples, tears pricking her eyes as she tried to imagine living her life as a woman without one—or both—of them. Doctor Calvin has seemed confident she wouldn't have to face such a decision but Shannon knew nothing was for certain besides the fact that she had cancer.

It was unimaginable, the cruelest of jokes for television's favorite darling. Shannon beat her hand on the shower wall and released a wail that sounded horribly pathetic in her own ears. She crumpled to the shower floor and finally allowed herself to feel the pain and sadness she'd been hiding for days. She wept for the loss she might have to endure and for her flailing hope she could truly face it all on her own.

When she could utter nothing more than a few weak hiccups, Shannon pulled herself up and finished rinsing residual soap from her skin before turning off the water. She exited the shower then towel dried her body and hair. With a dejected sigh, she padded into the bedroom and collapsed naked on the bed, needing just a little time to regroup before Jay arrived. She lifted the cover over her, closed her eyes then groaned when she heard soft knocking at her door.

Shannon eyed the clock on the nightstand to see how early Jay was, blinking in surprise when she saw he was on time. Had she really spent that much time in the shower?

It took much more effort than she'd thought it would to put on her silk robe and go to the door. She pulled it open and smiled despite her inner pain when she saw Jay's sexy grin. She couldn't help wondering what he'd think about her if he knew she was sick. "Hey, Celeb Hotel Chef."

"Hey, yourself." Jay kissed her forehead as he stepped into her suite. "I thought we were going out?"

"Would you mind terribly if we stayed in tonight?" Shannon cinched the tie on her robe at her side.

"Fine with me." Jay placed the bottle of wine he'd brought on her counter and took her into his arms. "Red, you had me worried as hell earlier. Are you sure you're okay? I was so worried about you."

"I know. I'm sorry." Shannon suppressed a shudder within his embrace. "Thank you for not making a big deal about it. I'm okay." She hugged him tighter. "I'm just glad you're here. Jay, I need you to make..." Her voice caught, emotions she dared not tap into rising unwanted to the surface. "I need you to..."

"Make love to you?"

Shannon nodded, lifting her face for his kiss, uncaring of the tears filling her eyes and spilling down her cheeks, wetting his face and hers as he tugged on her belt.

"Gladly, Red." Jay's voice was a husky whisper as her robe slipped from her body.

Shannon lifted up his T-shirt, helping him take it off. She splayed her fingers over his tight pecs, rubbed her palms over his biceps, admiring his muscles, needing to feel his strength to believe in her own. Jay took a condom out of his pocket before unbuttoning his dark tan chinos. Shannon pushed his pants down, caressed his cock through his underwear then yanked them down as well. "I missed you, Jay." She took the foil package from his hand, ripped it with her teeth and proceeded to sheath him.

Jay chuckled against her hair as he stepped out of his clothing and picked her up. Shannon wrapped her legs around his waist.

"I'm glad you missed me as much as I missed you. You're in my blood."

Shannon brushed her lips on his shoulder as he took her into the bedroom. She smiled up at him when he placed her on top of the sheets. Her gaze drifted over his hard body and cock and she held out her arms out to him. He came to her, moving between her legs to kiss her. Shannon moaned against his mouth, digging her fingers into his dreads, wanting the moment, the taste of him to last forever. His lips caressed and crushed hers, making her wetter and hungrier for him.

"Damn, you drive me so fucking crazy with need." Jay rose up on his knees to look down at her.

Shannon flushed further beneath his dark gaze, conscious of her nakedness and parted thighs braced against his. "Touch my breasts like you did the other night."

"Mmm. My pleasure." Jay gave her a sexy grin as he reached down to gently take both of her breasts into his hands. "I love these."

Shannon gasped as he teased her nipples, rolling the sensitive tips until they puckered and reddened beneath his fingers. She moaned with bliss when he lowered his frame to kiss the sides of her breasts, leaving her aching nipples alone for a few torturous moments. "Jay…" Shannon writhed under him, tugging on his hair, urging him to put his warm mouth back on her nipples.

"I got you, Red." Jay cupped one breast with both hands as he lovingly licked and kissed the tip.

Shannon arched her back, wanting him to take more of her between his lips, trying to imprint the heat of his mouth, the wetness of his tongue on her flesh in her memory forever.

Jay seemingly sensed her needs, circling her areola with his tongue before taking more of her breast into his mouth. Shannon mewled as he gave the other breast the same sweet treatment. Tears filled her eyes when he moved back to take hold of her still damp hair. She watched him through hooded eyes as he caressed her tender breasts with her tresses, shivering as the wet strands teased her skin. Shannon spread her thighs wider, inviting him, hoping he'd get her less than subtle clue.

Jay smiled down at her, released her hair and shifted his body over her, positioning himself to take her.

"Yes." Shannon gasped with delight as he slowly filled her. She dug her nails into his back, sucking in a breath as her body stretched to accommodate him.

"Breathe, Red."

Shannon drew in a ragged breath in response to Jay's husky command. She quivered when he was fully seated within her, kissing him as he began to move. Her passion tripled with each languid, deep stroke he gave her. She lost count of how many times his name fell from her lips as he reverently rocked her body.

"Sweet mercy."

His words were like a prayer, his cock inside her a beautiful blessing. Jay quickened his pace only when she fell silent, surrendering herself to the exquisite pleasure enrapturing her. Shannon let out a tiny sob, overwhelmed with ecstasy and by the way he'd worshiped her body with his own. She clung to him, moaning, reeling from the sensations ricocheting through her as Jay thrust faster within her. Shannon looked into his eyes, reveling in his groans. His measured thrusts became frenzied and Shannon whimpered from the depth of his final strokes as he came. She stopped him when he tried to move his body off hers, not wanting the love she'd felt from Jay to fade as her love for him welled up within her, undeniable and all-consuming.

* * * *

Jay stared down at Shannon as she slept, his heart swelling with the need to protect and love her. "Damn." He backed away from the bed when Shannon mumbled in her sleep, twisting in the sheets at the sound of his muted voice. Jay pulled on his chinos. He left the bedroom and padded through the sitting area. Not bothering to turn on any lights, he headed toward the kitchen, his head reeling with the realization he had fallen head over heels in love with Shannon.

She was everything he'd ever wanted or needed in a woman — kind, generous, sexy and insatiable. The show was over and soon she'd head back to California. Jay swore again as he opened the fridge in search for a beer. He found none. Taking out a bottle of water instead, Jay went over to the floor length windows, which offered a breath-taking view of the twinkling bright lights of The Strip. Falling for Shannon was the last thing he'd expected to happen, even after asking her if she wanted more.

Jay shook his head, amazed by the depth of his feelings and the sense of urgency to tell Shannon. He wanted to go back into the bedroom and wake her but she'd seemed so tired. Her behavior during the taping still concerned him, made him wonder if something really *was* wrong. As much as he'd wanted her, he'd planned just to take her to dinner and rein in his libido but all his good intentions had gone to sweet hell when she'd asked him to make love to her.

There was only one relationship, one woman he'd been crazy about in his past who Jay had ever felt he'd made love to. Shannon was the first woman to ask. Coming from any other lady the words might have freaked him out but coming from Shannon...it had felt right in his soul. What they'd just shared had touched a part of him he hadn't known existed, made him realize what had been missing in his life. Shannon made him feel whole.

Jay grinned as he drank his water. He couldn't wait to look into those bewitching emerald eyes and tell Shannon. Jay dug his cell out of his pocket to check for a message from Ari and frowned when he found nothing. With everything going on, he still hadn't had an opportunity to really talk with her about Ryder's troubling declaration. It seemed to Jay Ari was keeping a low profile, getting up early in the morning to rehearse, coming in late at night, making sure they didn't have any time to chat.

Setting the phone on the coffee table, Jay paused mid-sip when he heard a strange noise coming from the bedroom. He walked over the plush carpet back to the semi-dark room to check on Shannon. Another strangled noise coming from her direction prompted him to switch on the small lamp by the door, illuminating the space in soft light. Jay's scowl deepened when he saw Shannon sitting up in the bed clutching the covers to her face. "Shannon?"

Shannon lifted her face briefly to look at him, revealing her tear-streaked cheeks. "Jay."

He rushed over to her side, taking hold of her balled-up fists twisted in the sheets when she let out a sob. "What's wrong?"

Shannon shook her head, unable to speak as she wept. Her soft cries wrenched at Jay's heart. He wrapped his arms around her, disturbed that his touch seemed to make her cry harder, but he didn't let go. "Shannon..."

She clung to him but didn't answer. Devastated by whatever was causing her so much pain, Jay caressed her sweat-dampened hair. "Oh, baby, please. Please tell me what's wrong. Whatever it is, I want to help."

"Y-You can't help me. I-I *don't* want you to." Shannon struck her fist on his chest. "It's not *fucking* fair."

The vehemence in her voice set Jay further on edge. "What's not fucking fair?" He refused to acknowledge her statement of not wanting his assistance with whatever was bothering her.

"Oh, God." Shannon sagged against him then pulled herself from his embrace.

Jay watched her get up from the bed, naked and trembling. He stood too, picked her robe from the floor and wrapped it around her shoulders. "Shannon, tell me what's going on, right now."

"I didn't want to tell you." Shannon avoided his gaze as she put on the robe and cinched the belt around her waist. "I'm just so scared."

Jay took hold of her arms, preventing her from walking away. He racked his brain, trying to ascertain the source of her sadness. "Is it your mom? Is she sick?"

"No." Shannon finally met his gaze, her lashes spiky with tears. Her eyes were wide and empty. "I-It's me. I have breast cancer."

Nothing Jay had imagined Shannon would say could have prepared him for those four softly uttered words, or his visceral reaction. "Jesus." He released her and time stood still as Jay stared at her. The heartache ripping through him rendered him momentarily speechless. Flashbacks of his mother whispering the same words to him hit him like a sucker punch to the gut. Jay briefly rubbed his eyes, trying to physically blot out the images of her thin, ravaged body, the desperate look of pain in her eyes toward the very end of her fight to live.

"I'm sorry." Shannon turned her back to him. "I hadn't planned on sharing this tonight. I-I woke up from a bad dream and it all just hit me like a ton of bricks. I couldn't hold it in any longer."

Jay shook his head. "When did you find this out?"

"The day before yesterday." Shannon exhaled. "I had to make an appointment to get my birth control prescription filled. My doctor found a lump. I went in for a mammogram then a biopsy."

"You went through all of this without telling your mom...? Without telling me?" Jay blinked, surprised by the sting of tears clouding his vision. He placed his hand on Shannon's shoulder. "Red, you didn't have to go through that alone." Jay gritted his teeth, wanting to yell with frustration. *Not again.* He couldn't lose someone he loved to cancer again. Shannon was right. This *wasn't* fucking fair.

Shannon whirled on him. "I know what you've been through. I saw the look of horror and pain in your eyes when you talked about being there for your mother as she battled this disease. I am *not* going to put you through that again."

"Sha—"

They both froze as someone pounded on the hotel door.

"What the hell? Are you expecting someone?"

"No." Shannon cinched the robe to her belt tighter. "Will you go see who it is for me?"

Jay nodded and pivoted. He strode to the door, ready to send whoever it was on their merry way. He and Shannon still had many things to discuss. Jay pulled open the door, his gaze narrowing when he discovered the obnoxious knocker was Ryder.

"Sorry to disturb you two."

Jay raised an eyebrow at Ryder's uncharacteristically disheveled appearance. "Shannon's not feeling well—"

Ryder waved his hand. "I'm not here to see Shannon. I came looking for you. Ari's in trouble and she's not going to appear within seconds and talk her way out of it this time."

Jay tightened his grip tightened on the doorframe as he observed the tiny tic in Ryder's tense jaw. The man's concern for Ari went without saying. "She was gambling, wasn't she?"

Ryder gave him a curt nod, the steely glint of fury in his eyes evident. "Yeah."

"Fuck. Where is she? Is she hurt?"

"She's at that lounge where she performs." Ryder glanced at his phone. "We need to go now. I'll explain on the way."

"You didn't answer my second question."

Ryder leveled his gaze on him. "I don't think she's hurt." His tone expressed what his response didn't. The status of Ari's physical well-being could change in an instant.

"Just let me get dressed."

Ryder nodded. "We need to avoid the press still milling about in the lobby because of the show and after party. I have a vehicle at my disposal. I'll go get it, drive it around back and you can meet me by the southeast exit."

"Okay. I'll be there in less than ten minutes." Jay closed the door with another dark curse, rushing to gather his shirt and shoes. *What else can go wrong?*

Not bothering to put on a bra, Shannon tugged her T-shirt down as she walked into the sitting area. "Did

I just hear Ryder's voice?" She watched Jay grabbed his cell and keys off the coffee table.

"Yes." Jay paused for a second to look at her and the wild light in his eyes made her heart lurch. "Ari's got herself into something and Ryder and me are going to get her out of it. I'm so sorry for the timing of this."

"It's all right." Shannon crossed over to him. "You need to focus on Ari right now." She rubbed her hand on his forearm, managing a smile when he caressed her cheek with his finger.

"I want us to talk about everything."

"Okay." Shannon glanced at the door. "Is Ryder waiting outside?"

"I'm meeting him at a backdoor exit to avoid paparazzi."

"Well, I want to come with you guys."

"Red, no. No way."

Shannon held onto his arm when he started to move away. "Wait. I'll just go with you to the exit then."

"All right." Jay gestured at her attire. "You going in your sweats?"

"Yep."

Jay gave her a small smile. "Okay. Let's go."

Shannon followed him out of the door, picking up her pace to keep up with his long-legged strides. She pushed the button for the elevator, wishing she knew the right thing to say under their surreal circumstances. The elevator doors opened and Shannon's pulse quickened when Jay interlaced his fingers with hers as they stepped inside. She lifted her face to his after he pressed the proper button. Heart-felt emotions swept through her as he raised his hand to kiss her knuckles. She was touched by his need to comfort when he had to be in need of some himself.

The elevator doors opened again, they walked out in silence and Shannon was grateful the hallway was empty. They reached the exit where Ryder was to meet Jay and Shannon watched Jay push open the door. "Is he waiting for you?"

Jay shook his head as he peered out of the door. "Not yet. Damn. What's taking him so long?"

Shannon moved past him, stepping outside into the warm night. She drew in a deep breath, glancing at Jay when he joined her. "I know you must be worried sick."

"I am."

"Ari's a smart and resourceful woman. You have to believe she'll be okay until you get there."

"I'm trying to. Thank you." Jay gave her a quick squeeze. "I truly hope so."

Shannon glanced around his shoulder in the direction of the headlights that came into view. "Here comes Ryder now, I bet."

Jay shifted his body toward the SUV slowly approaching. "Finally." He frowned as the vehicle sped up. "Why is he driving so fast down this alley?"

Shannon didn't respond as the SUV stopped in front of them, relieved that Jay was on his way to help his sister. Her relief shifted to horror in nanoseconds as the passenger door was flung open. She heard Jay shout her name as two burly, unfamiliar men jumped out. Shannon screamed as one guy charged Jay, who instantly reacted, ducking in time to avoid a punch. Time slowed down for her while everything else seemed to speed up as Jay followed through with a punch of his own. Jay's assailant grunted with pain as the second man started in Shannon's direction. She backed up, screaming again when she saw Jay's attacker lift a Taser and make contact with Jay's abdomen.

Jay didn't appear to be initially affected by the crackle of electricity. He swung at the guy still jamming the device into him, connecting with the dude's jaw before falling to his knees.

Her own safety forgotten, Shannon called out Jay's name again and tears filled her eyes as she witnessed the grimace of pain on his face when the guy kicked him in the stomach.

"You're coming with us, doll."

Shannon attempted to hit the oversized thug but scratched him instead. Satisfaction surged through her upon seeing the streaks of blood on his face as he swore. She cried out when he caught her arm and wrenched it behind her back with just enough pressure to prevent further movement. Shannon gagged as a rag was pressed to her nose and mouth, and struggled to escape from the sickening smell and the man holding her back. She held her breath for as long as she could, struggling to free herself from her assailant at the same time. Her vision blurred as she lost her strength and inhaled deeply. Within seconds, her limbs refused to respond. Shannon groaned as she succumbed to the blackness beginning to overtake her. She closed her eyes, forgetting the last words of her prayer as she faded away.

Chapter Twelve

Jay winced as he slowly opened his eyes in pitch blackness. He resisted moving, not wanting to make his assailants aware that he was conscious. Blinking sluggishly, he realized they were being held in a room and he was bound to a chair. Jay quietly tested the bonds restraining him, his first foggy thoughts of Shannon. His vision adjusted within the dimly lit space. Jay almost called out when his gaze landed on Shannon, knocked out and tied to a chair across from him with her mouth taped shut.

Furious at his helpless state, Jay tried to part his lips then tasted the tape on his own lips. Pure rage ignited his blood, making him want to rail in his seat. He drew in a deep breath, knowing his and Shannon's life would depend on what he did next.

Jay stilled himself, ignoring the throbbing pain in his ribs. His vision was obscured in his left eye and the dull ache to his temple let him know he suffered from a black eye or worse. He tried to even out his breathing to avoid taking in the deep breaths he needed as he gingerly tugged on his restraints again in hopes of loosening them. Jay froze at the sound of a door opening. He closed his eyes and tried to slow his breathing even more as approaching footsteps to his left got closer.

"They're still out." The raspy voice registered with Jay. It belonged to one of the two men that had taken him and Shannon.

"Well, we'll wake them when that bitch gets here with our money."

Jay didn't recognize the voice but he heard the threat in his authoritative tone.

Raspy chuckled humorlessly. "Think she'll be able to come up with all of it?"

"Oh, she will. You stay here and watch 'em. They should be coming around any minute. I'll be back with either good or bad news for these two."

Jay balled his hands into a fist as Raspy laughed again. He wanted to get his fingers around both men's necks, and when he finally saw Ari... Jay tried to swallow the lump in his throat. God, he hoped she was all right. Was she tied up somewhere too? Maybe hurt? Jay mentally steeled himself. He couldn't entertain such dark thoughts now.

There was money in the bank and he had the prize money for winning *Celeb Hotel Chef*. Surely he had enough to cover Ari's debt. He just needed to tell these crooks he could pay it off.

Movement in front of him made Jay open his eyes just enough to peek at Raspy, who'd moved in front of Shannon. His pulse leaped into overdrive when the man reached out touch her hair.

"You sure are a pretty thing, aren't cha, doll?" Raspy dropped his hand to Shannon's breast, squeezed and Jay couldn't prevent the growl erupting from his throat. Raspy pivoted to look at him, striding forward, a menacing gleam in his dark eyes. "Mr. Tough Guy, you awake? I ain't never seen nobody take that electricity and keep standing." Raspy grinned. "Ain't so tough now though, huh?"

Jay glowered at him, wishing he could spit out the expletives on the tip of tongue. Both men shifted their attention to Shannon as she moaned. Jay's heart pounded against his chest as her dazed gaze rested on Raspy then locked on him. The fear in her eyes infuriated Jay as Raspy turned back to her.

"I couldn't wait for you to wake up." Raspy touched the side of Shannon's face and Jay struggled against his bonds as she turned her head away. "You left a nasty mark on me, Doll Face. Shouldn't I return the favor?"

Jay shifted in his seat, hating the helpless feeling sending his adrenaline into high gear as Raspy glanced at him over his shoulder.

"You got something to say, Mr. Tough Guy?" Raspy came over to Jay. "I do love good conversation."

Jay gritted his teeth as the man roughly ripped the tape off his mouth. "How much does my sister owe you guys?"

"Fifty thousand with change." Raspy shook his head. "Your sister is one helluva card player. Should've stopped while she was ahead. I'm always fascinated by those that play the game, win big then instead of walking away from the table, lose it all, plus some."

"I can get the cash." Jay glanced at Shannon. "Let us go and I'll get it for you."

"Hmm." Raspy scratched his stubbly chin. "I like your cooperative attitude but you'll have to talk that arrangement over with the boss man." He took out the cell from his pocket, punched some buttons then put it back. "Now where was I? Oh, yes...Doll Face." The man pivoted to look at Shannon, revealing the small knife in his grasp.

"Don't you *fucking* touch her."

Raspy howled with dark laughter, standing to the side of Shannon to assess Jay. "And to think I just complimented you on your cooperative attitude." He pointed to the reddened scratches on his ruddy face. "Look at what this bitch did. She gotta pay for that."

"I swear to God if you hurt her—"

"Shut the fuck up." Raspy yanked on Shannon's hair, angling her face to his as he pointed to Jay. "Don't say another fucking word or Doll Face suffers the consequences." He clucked his tongue as he caressed her cheek with the gleaming blade. "Such pretty, pretty skin. You know I'd kinda hate to mess it up? Maybe we can think of another way for you to make up for what you did? Hmm...whaddya think?"

Jay gritted his teeth so hard his jaw ached as Raspy released her hair to cup her breasts with both hands. He strained in his seat as the man cut her T-shirt in the front, exposing her nakedness. Shannon's frightened squeal sent a spike of fury so strong through Jay that he could barely see straight.

"Very nice." The thug traced the tip of his knife around Shannon's areola, pausing to glance at Jay, a wicked sneer on his face. "A scratch for scratch, right? How many I got on my cheek, Doll Face. *Look* at me."

Shannon visibly trembled as she followed the directive given.

Raspy counted the jagged marks on his cheek. "I got four."

Everything within Jay burned with wrath as Raspy dragged the tip of the blade over Shannon's nipple, causing her to whimper. Jay wanted to rip the man's arms off as he chortled. He had to do something…but what could he do strapped down the way he was? What could he say that wouldn't possibly enrage the man, making him injure Shannon just to prove a point? Jay had never felt more helpless or so murderous.

"Don't fret, Doll Face. It'll only be a scra—" Raspy straightened as the door behind him creaked. He stepped away from Shannon, shoving his knife into his back pocket as people approached.

"Jay!" The sound of Ari's voice filled Jay with some relief seconds before she wrapped her arms around his neck. "I'm so sorry."

"Family reunions later." The man Jay assumed was in charge pulled Ari back. He gestured at Jay with the revolver in his hand. "I heard you can get your hands on the fifty thousand your sister owes?"

"I can." Jay briefly glanced at Ari, his chest tightening again when he caught sight of the tears in her eyes and on her cheeks.

Boss man nodded. "Good, good. You have twenty-four h—"

The crunch of wood and metal behind Jay and Ari's shrill scream was deafening. Jay watched Ari drop to the floor. Seconds of chaos that felt like hours passed as Jay tried to discern from the stunned look on Shannon's face whether what was happening was positive or negative for them.

"This is the police. Everybody *freeze!*"

Relief flooded through Jay as five cops came into view and Raspy and Boss man scattered, disappearing out of his line of vision. Shots rang out and Jay froze, hating his inability to protect the two women he loved in the nightmarishly surreal situation. His gaze shifted to Ari crouched beside him then Shannon, his gut tightening with dread. There was some kind of scuffle taking place behind him as Jay met Shannon's tearful gaze. He wished he could hold her as she cringed. The cacophony of voices and unknown movement around him was maddening. "Hold on."

Shannon gave him the briefest of nods. He wanted to hear her voice but the tape on her mouth prevented him such comfort. Jay knew he'd never be able to erase the sight of her bound and gagged from his mind. He'd never be able to forgive himself for not being able to help her when she needed him most. Nothing would keep him from telling Shannon how he felt about her once they were safe.

* * * *

Shannon straightened her back, wishing she could stop trembling as she tightened her hold on the blanket that had been draped around her shoulders. She nodded with relief at the officer as he finally closed his notepad. He wanted answers that she didn't have.

"Do you need a ride back to your hotel?" Officer Quimby's gaze was warm as he studied her.

"Uh...I don't know." Shannon shifted her attention over Jay who was still speaking to another cop with his sister and Ryder. She wanted to talk with him but not with so many people milling around the chaotic scene. Her nerves were frayed and she didn't know how much longer she could pretend otherwise. "You know, on second thought, yes, please."

Officer Quimby nodded. "No problem. Give me a few minutes and I'll get you out of here. Thanks again for your help. We've finally got enough on Nico and Val to make sure a conviction sticks this time."

"No, thank you." Shannon returned the young man's smile before he walked off, fighting the urge to slouch, beyond exhausted. She sucked in a breath as Jay looked her way then headed over in her direction.

"Hey, Red."

Shannon tried not to tremble as Jay's gaze flitted over her.

"How are you holding up?"

Shannon shrugged. "Still standing."

Jay gently embraced her. "You're tough." He kissed the top of her head before she moved back.

"*Me?* You." Shannon's heart ached as she gazed at his swollen eye. "What did the paramedics say?"

"They want me to go with them to the hospital to confirm a couple of broken ribs and possible concussion."

"I'll go with you."

"No. You're exhausted. Go back to your room and rest, okay?"

Shannon searched his battered face. "Are you sure?"

"Yes. Ari's going to come with me. We need to talk anyway."

"All right." Shannon tried to shake of the conflicting emotions of guilt and relief washing over her at his suggestion. There was so much she wanted to say to him but now wasn't the time. She glanced over at Ari and Ryder still chatting with the policemen. "I'm so glad Ryder called the cops. Who knows what would've happened if they hadn't arrived when they did." Shannon wrapped her arms beneath her breasts, trying not to recall how scared she'd been when Val had touched her. "I still can't believe any of this happened."

"I know. Me either." Jay briefly shifted his gaze over to where his sister and Ryder stood. "I still feel like I'm missing some parts of the story."

"Well, thank God you don't have to pay Ari's debt. She's lucky you and Ryder came to her rescue."

Jay blew out a breath. "She's pretty shaken up. I don't think I've ever seen her like this. A part of me is glad. I hope what happened here tonight is enough to break her gambling addiction for good."

"Ms. Erby?"

Shannon and Jay turned to see Officer Quimby. "Yes?"

"A car is ready to take you back to your hotel. Officer Lawrence is standing over there." The cop gestured to another policemen. "He'll take you when you're ready."

"Thank you." Shannon looked at Jay as Officer Quimby strode off. "Please let me know what the doctor says?"

"I will. You'll be fine alone for a while?"

Shannon gave Jay a bright smile. "I'm tough, remember?" She raised her hand to his cheek, cradling his jaw in her palm for a moment before lifting her face for his kiss. Her pulse calmed some as Jay brushed his lips over hers. He stepped back and Shannon wanted to beg him not to leave her side.

"I'll call you as soon as I can."

"Okay." Shannon pivoted, blinking back fresh tears as she headed over to Officer Lawrence.

"We're going to take you out the side entrance of this lounge to avoid the press."

Shannon nodded at the cop, thankful for his help. She'd forgotten about the media. They'd love such a juicy story involving her and Jay, as the *Celeb Hotel Chef* winner. Shannon glanced behind her, saw Jay still watching her and lifted her chin in the same manner he'd done to her only a short time ago. His answering small grin comforted her as she faced forward, quickening her pace to keep in step with the policeman by her side.

Shannon welcomed the warm wind swirling around her once they were outside, grateful for the fresh air. The officer opened the passenger door to the squad car for her and Shannon thanked him as she got in. She settled into the seat, anxious to get back to her room to shower and change. A tremor swept over her as she touched her torn tee.

As terrified as she'd been, the ordeal had kept her from thinking about what she still had to deal with. Funny how her cancer scared her more than a loaded gun had. Shannon stared unseeing out of the window. She'd been fortunate to make it out of that situation alive and without a scratch. She could only hope her luck matched her will to survive going forward.

* * * *

Shannon awoke with a start, her heart racing, a tiny scream dying in her throat. Brushing her hair back, she sat up on the couch and tossed the throw to the side. She rubbed her eyes but could still see the images from her nightmare in which Val had wielded his knife over her, taunting her with it on her breasts as he laughed. Shannon picked up her cell to check the time, amazed she'd only been sleeping for an hour. It felt like she'd been struggling to escape from Val in her dreams for hours.

Her cell rang in her hand and she checked it, eager to hear back from Jay. She groaned when she saw it was her mother calling. "Hello?"

"Oh, my God, are you all right? How did this happen? *What* happened? Tell me everything, Shannon."

Shannon grimaced at the frantic, high-pitched tone in Clarion's voice. "Mum, I'm okay." She proceeded to give her mum the watered down version of what had transpired.

"I'm so glad you weren't hurt. I can't believe you didn't call to tell me about this."

"I didn't want to worry you. Honestly, I just got in. I showered and laid down to rest. How did you find out anyway?"

"Shannon, it's been on the news." Clarion sighed. "See? If you hadn't gotten involved with that chef, none of this would've happened."

"His name is *Jay*, Mother." Shannon rubbed her temple, in no shape or form ready to go toe to toe with her mum about Jay.

"Fine. If you hadn't gotten involved with *Jay*, you wouldn't have to deal with this less than favorable press coverage for somehow being present at a high-stakes gambling bust."

"Oh, please. I wasn't gambling. Jay wasn't gambling. I don't care what the media says about me, especially when I know it isn't true."

"You know the truth doesn't matter once the media puts a spin on things. All people will remember is your name tied to something seedy."

Shannon groaned. "You called to see if I was all right and I am. Mum, I'm exhausted. I'm going to have to talk to you later."

"But—"

"I'm sorry. There's another call coming in."

"*Shannon…*"

"Bye, Mother." Shannon ended the call. She slumped back against the couch cushions, feeling a modicum of guilt for the white lie she'd told about an incoming phone call. Her cell chimed in her hand and

Shannon lifted it, fully expecting to see her mum ringing again. Her mood lightened somewhat when she saw it was Jay as she answered the call. "Hello, Jay."

"No, it's Ari."

"Oh." Shannon frowned, surprised to hear Jay's sister on the other end. A sliver of trepidation crept up her spine. "Did something happen? Is Jay —"

"He's going to be fine. I was holding on to his phone for him while he was being X-rayed and I decided to call. My brother never changes the password on this damn thing. Anyway, I want to apologize for the predicament I put you both in tonight." Ari exhaled. "Shannon, I'm so sorry. I know that can't possibly make up for what you've been through but I hope you know I never intended to involve anyone else in my mess."

Shannon's gaze softened as Ari sniffled on the other end. "Ari, I know you didn't plan on your brother or me getting mixed up in any of this."

"Jay's been hurt. You... You were at the mercy of that thug. I don't think he'll ever forgive me for that."

"Jay loves you. He'll forgive you."

"What about you? I feel so guilty about all of this."

Shannon pushed back images of Val leering in front of her. "Stop beating yourself up. We've all been through enough tonight."

"You're so sweet to be so gracious to me still. I'm glad you're in Jay's life. He deserves some happiness and you make him smile."

"Thanks, Ari."

"You're welcome. Don't tell him this, but I've been glad he's had something else to focus on other than work or me. He hasn't been serious about any woman in a long time. Not since...since losing our mom."

Shannon sat up, wanting to ask the questions swirling in her head. "He told me about losing both of your parents. I'm so sorry, Ari."

"Thank you. Dealing with that kind of loss, twice, takes something out of you. Something you can't get back, especially in Jay's case. I think he tried to shield me from the uglier parts of our mom's struggle with cancer. He was my rock and I tried to be his when he'd let me."

"It sounds like the two of you leaned on each other."

Ari exhaled. "Uh, oh. Here comes, Jay. I meant to hang up before being spotted."

"Ari, what are you doing on my phone?"

Shannon smiled at the sound of Jay's voice in the background, more convinced by his irritated question to Ari that he was all right than her stating he was.

"Gotta go, Shannon. Thanks for being so sweet."

"Thanks for calling, Ari." Shannon heard some commotion then grinned as she caught snatches of their conversation on how Ari had obtained the password for Jay's phone.

"Shannon? You still there?"

"I'm here. Hi."

"Hey. I'm sorry it took so long to call. It took longer than I thought to get checked out."

"It's okay." Shannon relaxed her posture, happy to hear his voice. "What did the doctor say?"

"Two bruised ribs, one black eye but no concussion."

"Geez."

"Yeah. Could've been worse."

Shannon tightened her grip on her phone, knowing that was the understatement of the year. "Is Ari still there with you?"

"No. She just left with Ryder. I'm heading back to the hotel now. How are you?"

Shannon worried her bottom lip, trying not to picture all of the other horrifying turns the evening could've taken.

"Red?"

"I need you."

"I'm on my way, baby."

Relieved, Shannon set her phone beside her on the couch. She drew in a shuddering breath, blinking back tears as parts of her conversation with Ari replayed in her mind. She knew it was selfish but she wanted Jay to be her rock too. It wasn't fair to ask and she wouldn't. Jay had dealt with enough.

One more night together, to say goodbye. Shannon rubbed her tired, damp eyes. Jay would help her sleep and that was exactly she needed, especially with a television interview taking place in the morning. Shannon smoothed her mussed hair as she rose from the sofa to splash cold water on her face. She ignored the niggling voice questioning her on what she planned to do about the rest of what were sure to be sleepless nights.

Chapter Thirteen

Jay reached for Shannon the moment she closed the door behind them. He wrapped his arms around her, loving the way she leaned into him and embraced him back. Jay could feel all of her delicate feminine curves beneath the simple blue negligée she wore as she trembled against him. He held her tighter for a moment before briefly dipping his head to capture her lips in a tender kiss. "Hi."

"Hi." Shannon looked up at him and the unshed tears shimmering in her eyes tore at his heart.

"I'm sorry I had to leave you alone for a while."

Shannon shrugged. "Couldn't be helped." She hugged him again. "I'm just happy you're here now."

"Me too. What a fucking nightmare. When I saw you bound to that chair—"

"Shh…" Shannon pressed her finger to his lips. "I don't want to talk about it. I want you to make me forget about the past five hours. Do you think you can do that?"

"I'll damn sure try." Jay grinned as Shannon took him by the hand and led him toward the bedroom. "I need to take a quick shower first."

"Real quick?"

Jay kissed her nose, amused by her pouty face. "Very quick." He pulled off his shirt, stripped out of his pants and underwear, aware of Shannon's gaze drifting over him.

"Your ribs..." Shannon looked up at him. "I'm sorry. I forgot that you're hurt. Maybe sex isn't the best idea right now. Aren't you in pain?"

"A little." Jay stepped in front of her. He smoothed his hands over her shoulders. "But I want you. Being with you now is the only way I want this hellish night to end."

"I don't know, Jay." Skepticism colored Shannon's voice. "Physical exertion can't be good for you right now. Did the doctor give a prescription for painkillers?"

"He did. I don't want to take them." Jay wrapped his arm around her back. "Woman, you're the only medicine I need."

"Mmm...will the water affect this?"

Jay sucked in a tight breath as Shannon wrapped her fingers around his hard cock. "Not a chance." He secured his dreads with a lock of his own hair.

"Good." Shannon released her hold on him. "Hurry."

Jay chuckled as he pivoted. He deposited his clothes on the bed then made a beeline to the bathroom. The half circle shower was nicer than his, with a glass door and a massaging shower head. Jay turned on the shower, adjusted the water and got in. He selected the complimentary bar of soap and lathered his body, glad to at least physically wash away the day.

Rinsing the soap from his skin, Jay gritted his teeth when he touched his abdomen. His ribs were sore as hell. He could deal with the pain, forget it even once he slipped inside Shannon. Jay turned beneath the stream and his cock twitched when he saw Shannon, naked, leaning against the doorframe with her green eyes locked on him. The desire in her eyes was evident despite the steamed up glass. Rock hard once again, Jay turned off the water. He opened the shower door, stepped out and Shannon handed him a towel.

"Feel better?"

"Not yet." Jay briskly dried off then tossed the towel over the towel rack. He stepped toward Shannon and took hold of her hand. "Can you help me with that?"

"Absolutely." Shannon pulled him forward, tossing him a saucy grin over her shoulder as they entered the bedroom. "I promise to take it easy on you."

"Uh huh." Jay grinned as she giggled and got on the bed. He reached for her feet and kissed her toes.

"More, more, more."

"You want what I want." Jay sat on the bed, patted his lap and Shannon moved to straddle his thighs. He nipped the side of her neck, enjoying her delighted gasp as he caressed her back. "We need a condom."

"You left one on the nightstand." Shannon stretched to reach for it.

She tore the foil packet with her teeth, and Jay took it from her as Shannon perched her knees on the bed. Jay loved the way she squeezed his legs with her soft thighs. Jay groaned as she caressed his cock, all his injuries forgotten. He sheathed himself beneath her steady hungry gaze. "Take what you need, Red."

Shannon responded by positioning herself over his dick and Jay groaned with pleasure as she slowly took him in. She stopped just short of taking every inch and

Jay rewarded her by kissing her breasts. Jay sucked her nipples, reveling in her soft moans as she began to move on top of him. Jay gritted his teeth, the sweet sensations of her warm, slick sheath increasing as Shannon got wetter. He lifted his mouth from her breasts to nip at her neck as he caressed her back with his fingers.

"Oh, Jay…" Shannon tilted her head back and her hair brushed against his hands.

"Yes, love." Jay kissed her lips, deepening it when she rocked faster on his lap. She let out a blissful moan before leaning forward to meet his gaze. The passion sparkling in her eyes made Jay's cock thicken even more.

Shannon mewled as she placed her hands on his shoulders and increased her pace. "I'm going to come."

Her husky declaration elicited another groan of delight from Jay as she cried out. The walls of her pussy milked his dick, taking Jay closer to the edge. Hey held her in his arms, steadying her trembling body as he took over the rocking motion she'd established. Jay gave up trying to hold back his orgasm. He welcomed the intense whorls of ecstasy cresting within him, coming hard as Shannon clung to him. Jay gradually slowed his movements then stopped.

"So good." Shannon nuzzled the column of his neck.

"Mmm." Jay brushed his lips against her hair, listening to the sound of their harried breathing. He groaned again when Shannon tightened her sheath around his ultra-sensitive, still hard cock.

"You can feel that?" Shannon gave him a lazy, sated grin as she reached out to touch his hair.

"Yes—" Jay growled against her neck when she repeated the action. "Minx." He smiled as she laughed, content to keep her in his arms, connected to him forever. "Shannon, I love you."

Shannon stilled on Jay's lap, supremely conscious of him deep inside her. The physical connection matched the one she felt in her heart but she was shocked by his unexpected declaration. Joy flooded through her as she leaned back to meet his steady gaze. "What?"

"You heard me, but I'll say it again. I love you, Red."

"Oh, Jay…" Shannon dropped her face from his, her happiness fading as she thought about what might lie ahead for him if he continued to be with her. She couldn't be the one to put him through that kind of emotional stress again.

"Tell me you don't feel the same."

Shannon slowly lifted up off Jay, sucking in a breath at the tiny blissful aftershocks zinging through her as she did. She wanted nothing more than to utter those three words back to Jay as she turned from him in search of her robe.

"Shannon, answer me."

Shannon snatched her robe off the chair by the wall as she whirled around to face Jay. "We both said we wanted more but I wasn't expecting this." It was the truth and she could look him in the eye as she spoke. She cinched her robe around her body as Jay got up. Her heart thumped against her ribcage as she watched him dispose of the condom in the receptacle near the bed. She stood her ground as he approached her, heedless of his naked state, and her stomach fluttered. Even in the midst of heartache, his male beauty thrilled her.

"I wasn't expecting to fall for you either but it happened and I'm glad."

Shannon shook her head. "No."

"No?"

Shannon ignored the shards of pain ripping through her as Jay stared at her. "This isn't what I wanted." Guilt and longing made her cross her arms as her gaze drifted over his muscled chest.

"You mean *I'm* not who you wanted to love, right?" Jay winced as he bent to pick up his pants that had slipped off the bed to the carpet.

Shannon shivered as Jay put his pants on, reacting to the edge in his voice. "It's more complicated than that." She watched him fasten his pants. "I've got my career...you've got yours. We live in different cities. Let's face it...we weren't trying to build a future together."

"Red, I would like to do just that — with you."

The concern and love she heard in his voice and saw on his handsome face almost broke her resolve to break things off. Jay took a step toward her, and Shannon moved back, tears blurring her vision as he frowned.

"Shannon, talk to me. What's really going on with you? Is this because of the cancer?"

Shannon flinched, still unaccustomed to hearing that word in relation to her. "No."

"Are you sure?"

"Jay, the show is over and I'm going to go home to deal with this." Shannon crossed her arms beneath her breasts, trying to stem the tremors coursing through her.

"Who will be there for you?"

"I have friends." Another lie, but she couldn't tell him the truth. "My mum can be a pain but she'll support me."

Jay scoffed. "Have you even told her about your cancer yet?"

"Stop saying that word!" Shannon turned away from him, blinking back tears. She held back a sob when she felt Jay's hands on her shoulders.

"Red...I'm sorry. I can't imagine how difficult it must be to hear it."

Shannon pivoted to face him, overwhelmed with her love for him and his understanding of her. "I... It's okay." It wasn't. Nothing was and Shannon couldn't see how it would ever be again.

"Shannon, I want to be there for you. I know you have strong feelings for me —"

"I *don't* love you." Her sharp words seemed to echo in the room as Jay dropped his hands from her shoulders. The silence that followed her lie was deafening. Shannon could almost visualize the wall going up between them as her heart twisted in a million directions. The hurt in Jay's eyes matched the pain ripping through her, making it hard to breathe.

"You don't love me." Jay blinked as if still trying to process the incredulity of her declaration.

"I-I don't love you."

Jay slowly nodded. "Okay then."

"Jay —"

He held up his hand. "Nothing more needs to be said. How soon do you think you'll head back to California?" Jay walked away from her to pick up his shirt.

"I'm not sure yet." Shannon brushed away the tears on her cheeks, feeling like she was on the verge of a total breakdown.

"I'd like to see you before you go." Jay's expression was unreadable as he put on his shirt.

"Okay." Shannon bit the inside of her cheek to keep from screaming as she followed Jay out of the bedroom. She drew in shallow breaths as Jay slipped his feet into his leather thongs then proceeded to the door. It took all of her self-control to remain silent and impassive as he pivoted to look at her.

"I hope you'll at least keep me abreast of what's going on with you once you go back home, Shannon." Jay gave her a tight smile. "Always friends?"

Shannon managed to nod as he opened the door and stepped out into the hall. She struggled to keep her arms at her sides as Jay bent to brush his lips against her cheek.

"Goodbye, Shannon."

Shannon didn't trust herself to speak. She cried out within herself as Jay turned and strode away. She released the handle from her grasp, sinking to the floor as the door clicked close. Silent sobs racked her body as she tried to take comfort in the reasoning behind her decision to let the love of her life walk out of the door, but she found none as she forced herself up onto her feet.

* * * *

Shannon smoothed a hand over her yellow dress then fixed a smile on her face as she walked out on set. She waved to the crowd applauding as she took her seat next to Jessica Davis, an anchor for a popular day-time entertainment news program.

"Welcome, Shannon. It's so good to have you on the show today." Jessica nodded as the audience clapped. "Girl, I love that dress. Who are you wearing?"

Shannon rattled off the designer's name as she placed one leg over the other and her red stilettos shimmered beneath the lights.

"Ooo...those heels are to die for too."

"Thanks, Jessica." Shannon grinned as more applause erupted in the studio.

Jessica patted her knee. "Well, congratulations on another successful show. *Celeb Hotel Chef* garnered high ratings."

"Thanks so much." Shannon nodded at the cheering people again. "It's been a dream come to true to host the show."

"Speaking of hosts...my, my, *my*, is your co-host a handsome one." Jessica winked at the audience as they cheered. "I can admit I was hoping some sparks would fly between the two of you but surprise, surprise...the electricity was truly between you and Chef Dax."

Shannon offered her television smile. "What makes you think that, Sharon?"

"Oh, please" — Jessica waved her hand at her — "the chemistry between you two is undeniable. Am I right, audience?" She nodded as the crowd noisily backed her up. "What's up with you two?"

"I'm so excited for Chef Dax. He's amazing at what he does and I know winning the title of Celeb Hotel Chef will only propel his already stellar career to greater heights."

Jessica gave her a coy look. "How nice, but you didn't exactly answer my question."

"Chef Dax is a great friend of mine." Shannon faced one of the cameras pointing her direction. "I wish him the best in all his future endeavors and I'm quite sure he reciprocates my sentiments."

"All right." Jessica shrugged at her audience. "I can see we're not going to get more out of you *that* subject, but what can you tell us about that police bust you were involved in yesterday?"

Shannon raised an eyebrow, ready to recite the exact words her publicist had instructed her to say. "I'm not at liberty to discuss the details of an ongoing case, Jessica. I'm sure you can understand." She fixed a grin on her face as the crowd murmured their disapproval.

Jessica shook her head. "From all accounts, it sounds like you were lucky to escape unscathed."

"Well," Shannon chuckled. "I *am* glad to be here to talk to you to today."

Jessica wagged one long, lacquered nail in her direction. "You are too much. You managed to evade all my questions. Can you at least give me an answer as to whether there will be another season of *Celeb Hotel Chef*?"

"There will be." Shannon beamed at the enthusiastic crowd. "Look for season two to kick off this spring, Jessica."

"That's great news! I'll be tuning in. Shannon. Thanks for joining us this morning."

"My pleasure."

"Tell, Chef Dax I said *hello*." Jessica grinned as members of her audience snickered.

"*You're* the one who's too much." Shannon shook her head as Jessica laughed. She waved at the crowd, exhaling as the red lights on the cameras in front of her turned off. After thanking Jessica for the interview, Shannon left the set. She hurried to the exit she'd instructed her driver to wait for her at, not breathing a real sigh of relief until she was seated in the limo.

Her cell vibrated and Shannon lifted it to see a text from her mum, complimenting her on her choice of outfit. Shannon pushed the device back into her purse with a weary sigh. She settled into the leather seat and closed her eyes, weary from yet another sleepless night. Her eyes felt gritty and her heart ached as her thoughts drifted to Jay.

His good morning text had surprised her and bolstered her spirits. He'd even wished her luck on her interview. She'd thanked him for his message and sent along the same well wishes for his day. There had been so much more she wanted to say but Jay was right...at this point, there was nothing left to be said except what she couldn't say.

Shannon sighed as the limo pulled into the parking lot for the hospital. Her tummy flipped and flopped as she looked up at the building in which she'd been given the news that had inexorably changed her life. She wished Jay were accompanying her to her doctor's appointment. His calming presence was exactly what she needed at the moment.

Shannon comforted herself with the hope she'd done the best thing for them both by letting him go. Leaning on him would've proved disastrous for her emotionally if their relationship had floundered beneath the stress involved, and she wouldn't have been able to deal with causing him any undue heartbreak either.

Shannon toyed with the gold bracelet on her wrist as the car came to a stop. She tried to swallow the lump in her throat as the c-word reverberated in her mind. Protecting the one she loved had to count for something in her fight against cancer. Shannon prayed her heart-wrenching selfless act would earn her some credit in the karma department.

Chapter Fourteen

Jay unbuttoned the collar of his uniform as he shut the door to his office. He'd snapped at two of his sous chefs and nearly barked at Bret for messing up the new martini he'd shown him how to make earlier. Jay rubbed his gritty eyes and considered calling home to see if Ari had moved off the couch. He was concerned about her. Whatever had been going on between her and Ryder appeared to have fizzled out. Once again out of work, Ari seemed to have fallen into some kind of depression, which was totally unlike her. She always bounced back from her failed misdeeds.

Jay took his cell out of his pocket and texted his sister a silly greeting. He waited a few seconds for a response then set it on his desk as he sat down. He owed his lack of concentration and frayed patience to his sister and a certain redhead he'd been trying to push out of his mind for weeks. Four weeks and six days, to be exact.

He kept thinking the more time that passed the easier it would get to ignore the hole in his heart, but every day it felt like it was getting bigger. Jay shuffled through invoices, his mind on Shannon. He still couldn't believe how things had gone down between them. Rejection had been the last thing he'd expected after declaring his love. He'd been so certain she'd felt the same way. It had taken considerable restraint not to grab her, take her into his arms and kiss her until her lips echoed the depth of emotion he'd seen in her teary eyes.

His heart ached every time he replayed their last moments together in her hotel room. He knew she had a lot to deal with, suspected she was afraid to trust in his support and he hadn't wanted to press her. He'd thought giving her some time to miss him, to want...hell, *need* him would drive her out of the cocoon she'd seemingly enveloped herself in and that she'd reach out to him. Almost five weeks and their only communication had been when he'd prompted a response to his text in which he'd inquired about her well-being. Her short three word reply of *I'm fine. You?* had grated on his nerves.

How could she be fine when his world felt incomplete?

Jay slammed his fist down on his desk as the ever-present question in his mind echoed in his head. How could Shannon not love him when he loved her so fucking much?

It didn't make any sense and with every day that passed he realized he needed to move on. Jay swore under his breath. He had no clue how he to do it, how to forget Shannon. Jay sat up in his chair upon hearing two knocks on his door. "Come in."

Mallory, one of the hosts on staff, popped her head in. "Chef Dax, there's a Ryder Stevens here to see you?"

Jay raised an eyebrow. "Okay, send him on back. Thanks, Mallory."

Mallory nodded with a grin before walking off. Jay tapped a pen on his desk, wondering what the man could want. He hadn't seen him since the night of gambling bust when Jay had thanked him for getting the cops involved. Jay often thought of how differently that night could've turned out if Ryder hadn't called in the authorities. He still felt Ryder knew more about what Ari had been doing than he'd ever let on. Jay pushed those thoughts from his mind as Ryder knocked on his door frame.

"Hey, Ryder."

"What's up?" Ryder came into his office and closed the door.

"You tell me." Jay gestured to the chair nearby his desk and Ryder took a seat.

"Two things, actually."

"Shoot."

Ryder crossed his long, jean-clad legs at the ankles. "I've offered Ari a job. I've recently taken over ownership of my parents' exclusive resort in Florida. She'd perform five nights a week. I've offered her a competitive wage and she'd have room and board. She's skeptical about taking the position but I think you'd agree with me that her getting away from this place for a while would be a good thing."

"It would be. I do agree." Jay frowned. "Ari didn't mention any of this to me."

Ryder shrugged. "I think she wanted time to come to a decision first."

"You want me to convince her to take the job?"

Ryder grinned. "Well, Ari values your opinion. I've given her a deadline on accepting my offer by tomorrow and I suspect she will come to you about it."

"Got it. I do think this would be a great opportunity for Ari."

"It will." Ryder leaned forward and placed his elbows on his knees. "I've got some time between gigs and I plan to personally oversee the renovations I have in mind to take my parents' side project to the next level. I give you my word I will make sure your sister is taken care of. She'll be so busy, she won't have any time to get into mischief or gamble."

Jay nodded, already sold on the idea. "Thanks, Ryder. I trust you."

"Likewise, which is why I feel compelled to tell you that Shannon didn't show up for an important meeting with Shawn Rill and me this afternoon. She didn't call to cancel, nor after not being present." Ryder shook his head. "I haven't known her long but this seems totally unlike her. I know you two are...were seeing each other. Have you talked to her?"

"Not recently." Jay tightened his jaw, every fiber in his being telling him that something was off.

"I called her earlier. Got voicemail." Ryder shook his head. "My concern turned to worry when I got an unexpected call from her mother."

"Clarion called you?"

Ryder nodded. "Said she got my number from Shawn and was wondering when I'd last chatted with Shannon this past week. She tried to play it easy and breezy but I could tell that was just an act for me."

Jay bit back a curse as he reached for his phone and proceeded to call Shannon. He listened to it ring, his frustration and unease rising when he too got her voicemail. "No luck."

Ryder blew out a breath. "Think something is wrong?"

"I'm going to find out." Jay wondered if Shannon had finally shared the news about her illness with her mother.

"Going to call again later?"

"I'm going to fly out there. What's Clarion's number?"

Ryder punched buttons on his phone then shared the digits.

"Thanks, I'm going to get Shannon's address from her mother." Jay stood as Ryder did and shook his hand. "I'll also do my best to persuade my sister to give Florida a chance. God knows, I haven't gotten a good night's rest since she's been in Sin City."

Ryder went to the door and opened it. "She might not want to leave."

"If I have to put her on the plane myself, she'll go."

Ryder chuckled. "Keep me posted about Erby."

"Will do." Jay closed the door, went back to his desk and grabbed his cell.

Ten minutes later he had booked a flight on the next plane leaving for Los Angeles. He dialed Clarion next, impatiently tapping his pen on the desk as he waited for her answer.

"Hello?"

"Hello, Clarion. This is Jay Dax."

"Jay? Oh, hello. This is a surprise."

"How are you?"

"I'm well. Thank you for asking." Clarion cleared her throat. "I'm sure you didn't call to small talk. Something's wrong, isn't?"

Jay realized in an instant Clarion knew nothing about Shannon's cancer. "Clarion, your daughter—"

"What's the matter with Shannon?"

Jay hesitated for a second, torn with whether to hide or share Shannon's secret. It didn't seem right for him to be the one to tell Clarion and yet he wasn't comfortable lying either.

"Jay? I know something is going on with her. She's been more distant, moodier than usual...I can hardly get her to return my calls. We don't have the closest of relationships but she normally calls to check on me." Clarion sighed. "I'm worried. *Please* tell me what's going on. Did she lose her job or something?"

"There *is* something going on with her but it has nothing to do with work."

"Oh, good." Clarion voice had brightened. "All right then, what is it?"

"I think she should be the one to tell you."

"She probably won't." Clarion chuckled. "She hates to share anything negative going on in her life with me."

Jay held back from saying Shannon's lack of disclosure was probably due to her feeling less than supported in the past. "I need Shannon's address. I'd like to surprise her, cheer her up if I can."

"Okay but why do I get the feeling you're doing everything you can not to tell me what the hell is going on with my daughter? I want to know. You want the address..."

Jay gritted his teeth, annoyed at Clarion's little blackmail innuendo. She left him no choice. "Clarion, Shannon..."

"Shannon what?"

"Shannon has breast cancer."

Clarion gasped. "*What? No.* Not my Shannon."

"It's the truth. She was diagnosed while in Las Vegas before the show ended. Her doctor here was confident the cancer could be eradicated with surgery and chemo. Shannon told me she wanted to go home for treatment and I was under the impression she was going to share the news with you."

"Oh, my, God. Sh-she didn't tell me. Why didn't she *tell* me? I had no idea."

Jay felt compassion for Clarion as she sniffled. "I think she wanted to deal with it on her own. I wanted to be there for her too. I'm flying out in an hour. Please give me her address." Jay quickly wrote down the information Clarion gave him. "I know you probably want to go to her—"

"She didn't want me involved. I should respect her wishes."

"Jesus, Clarion." Jay paused a beat, trying to bank the furious edge in his tone. "She needs you, whether she admits it or not." He shook his head with frustration, the irony of his declaration as it pertained to him not lost. Jay prepared to say goodbye when Clarion remained silent. Seconds stretched as Jay considered the sad fact that saying anything more seemed pointless.

"Maybe you're right." Clarion huffed. "But it's clear to me she needs you more right now. I'm glad you're going to her. I will make sure to come see Shannon tomorrow."

"I think that would be great." Jay stood, pleased Clarion was willing to swallow her hurt and pride.

"Please let me when you've arrived safely, Jay."

Jay promised to do so then hung up. "What's going on with you, Red?" He exited his office to tell his staff about his trip before leaving. He knew Shannon would most likely be pissed he'd told Clarion about her situation. There was a great chance she'd be mad as hell to see him period, but he didn't care as long as he saw with his own eyes that she was all right. Jay picked up his pace, in a hurry to be on his way. He prayed Shannon was okay. Not knowing was pure hell.

* * * *

Shannon thanked her doctor, her forced smile fading the moment the physician left her alone in the doctor's office. She drew in a deep breath then gritted her teeth, bracing herself against the wave of nausea hitting her. Her doctor had seemed pleased she could prescribe something to help combat the common side effect. Shannon wondered if there was something the physician could give that would make her feel human again as she slid off the examination table.

She caught sight of her reflection in the small mirror above the sink and paused. Her beautiful, shoulder-length red locks, the part of her she'd always treasured, were long since gone. She'd chopped her hair two weeks after beginning her chemotherapy, when it had started to fall out. Now she had an ultra-short pixie cut that she had been considering covering up with a longer wig. She didn't recognize the woman in the mirror, felt detached from everything, everyone, even herself.

It was her fault. She knew that. It had been her choice not to tell her mum about what she was dealing with and her decision to break things off with Jay. Shannon mechanically pulled on her aquamarine A-line style dress, barely glancing at her cell as it chimed yet again to alert her of voice messages she hadn't listened to. She didn't want to hear what Shawn or Ryder had to say about missing today's meeting in Vegas about the second season of *Celeb Hotel Chef*. She planned to call Shawn back later and apologize, knowing he'd read her the riot act, no matter what excuse she gave him, and she had no intentions of telling him the truth. She hadn't informed him or Ryder about her cancer, didn't want them to suspect she was incapable of juggling her career.

Shannon sighed, recognizing they probably already questioned her competence by being absent. The truth was that she'd forgotten to look at her calendar, her nerves frayed over what news she'd learn from her doctor's visit. It seemed, according to her lab tests, that her treatment was working. Her doctor had told her to celebrate the good news in one breath and to be ready for a possible setback in the next. Shannon didn't know what to feel other than fear. The fact remained that she wasn't out of the woods yet when it came to the disease that had taken hold of body.

Exhaling, Shannon took her phone out of her purse to see who else had called. Her eyes widened with surprise and her heart somersaulted when she saw Jay's number. He hadn't tried to contact her since she'd given him some cryptic reply to his inquiry about how she was doing. Being honest had seemed out of the question.

Tears filled her eyes as she lifted the device to her ear to hear his message to give him a call back. As much as she wanted to, Shannon instead shoved her phone back into her purse and exited the room. She acknowledged the nurses and receptionist as she left the oncology suite, drawing in a deep breath the moment she was outside. She missed Jay terribly, had thought about calling him several times in the past few weeks. Her determination not to involve him had weakened her spirits in a way she refused to quantify.

Shannon walked to the limo awaiting her in front of the building, greeting her driver as he opened the door for her. She slid into her seat and closed her eyes as he shut the door. Shannon turned her face to toward the sunlight, savoring the warmth on her skin. She yawned as the vehicle started to move, exhausted by her recent treatment and another night of tossing and turning. All she wanted was a shower and her covers pulled up over her head.

"Ms. Erby?"

Shannon jumped when her driver's voice interrupted her erotic dream of Jay. "Y-Yes?" She blinked and focused on Clyde's face in the rearview mirror.

"I'm sorry I startled you, but we've arrived at your place."

"Thanks, Clyde." Shannon straightened in her seat as he raised the partition between them.

A few seconds later, Clyde opened the door for her. Shannon got out of the car and thanked Clyde again. She ignored the pretty flowers in full bloom as she walked up the few steps leading to the gated fence which allowed access to her tri-level residence. With a weary sigh, she slid her key into the lock and entered her home

Shannon disarmed her security system then tossed her purse on the small table by her door. She went to her bedroom, stripped out of her clothing then padded to her bedroom, eager to shower. Minutes later, she stepped beneath the warm stream, eager to wash off the day. She scrubbed her skin until it stung then gingerly rubbed her fingers over the tiny scar along the side of her breast where the cancerous lump had been removed. The flesh felt raised and foreign beneath her touch, still a little tender. Shannon dropped her hand from her breast then lifted her face to rinse off any residual soap.

She shut off the water then stepped out of the shower. Shannon towel dried off without looking in the mirror. It only took five minutes to dry her shorn head, something she appreciated when she was this tired. Shannon turned off the blow drier and ruffled her hair, ready to get back into bed and shut out the world.

Shannon went into her bedroom, opened her dresser and took out an ice blue negligée. She pulled it overhead then froze in surprise when her doorbell rang. She didn't get any visitors and her mother wouldn't come unannounced. Shannon had absolutely no idea who would be at her door. She hurriedly smoothed the silk down over her body and walked to the intercom by her door. "Hello?"

"Shannon? It's Jay."

Shannon's mouth parted in a wide 'O', words failing her. Jay was here? Shock rendered her speechless. She couldn't believe he'd flown to California and was actually less than twenty feet away. How did he even know her address?

"Shannon?"

"J-Jay?"

"Yes. Please let me in."

Shannon trembled as she pushed the button to allow him entrance, the depth and irony of his request not lost on her. She waited for him to reach her door, her emotions scattered across the board. Her heart thudded against her chest with joy and dismay as Jay knocked. How dare he sneak up on her like this? Shannon reached up to touch her hair as she twisted the knob. What would he think when he saw her with no makeup and her new unwanted do?

With a shuddering breath, Shannon pulled the door open, and Jay stepped inside her foyer. Tears sprang to her eyes the instant her gaze connected with Jay's. She trembled as he looked at her, annoyed and overwhelmed with how happy she was to see him.

"Oh, Red." Jay's voice was husky as he held out his arms.

His voice, his presence squashed whatever else she was feeling except for her desire to be back in his embrace. Shannon let out a small sob as she went to him. She began to weep as Jay hugged her, comforted by his hard body pressed on hers, feeling safe for the first time in weeks. "D-Don't let me go."

"I won't, baby. I won't."

Shannon sagged against Jay as her strength gave out. He held her tighter as she sobbed and she relied on him, all her reservations forgotten.

Chapter Fifteen

Jay picked Shannon up and carried her over to the plush, oversized chair by her couch. He sat down, taking care to be gentle with her as he cradled her in his arms, her fragility and beauty crushing him. "Shh... It's going to be okay." Jay knew as he spoke the words he'd do everything humanly possible to make sure it was. He blinked back the tears in his own eyes as Shannon clung to him, wishing he'd come to her sooner.

His heart ached as she cried. The only thing he could do was hold through the storm of tears racking her body. She felt lighter on his lap and the weight loss concerned him, but it was the emptiness in her eyes that troubled him the most. Jay wanted to tell her how much he loved her but didn't want her to go skittish on him like she had last time. He was okay with not voicing the depth of his feelings for her if that was what it took to be a part of her life. Jay raised his hand to her head and smoothed her hair. He pressed kiss after kiss on her short locks until she slowly began to quiet.

Jay noticed a box of tissues on the table nearby. He reached for them, pulled out a few and passed them to Shannon. Jay rubbed her back as she took them, grinning with relief when she blew her nose.

"I'm sorry." Shannon lifted her face from his chest to look at him. "I know I must look a mess." She reached and touched her shortened tresses. "My hair...I didn't want you to see me like this."

"Stop." Jay brushed his lips against her damp cheek. "I see *you* and you're beautiful." He took hold of her chin when she shook her head. "Yes, you are, and I love this hairdo on you."

Shannon gave him a wobbly smile. "Really, Jay?"

"Yes." Jay released his hold on her face to tease her hair. "It's sexy and it draws attention to your elegant bone structure."

"Thank you."

"You're welcome.

"I want to believe you." Shannon dropped her face from his.

"You can, Red."

"I don't recognize myself anymore." Shannon shuddered on his lap. "I don't trust any of my emotions.

"I won't pretend to know what you've been going through physically or emotionally but I want you to trust *me* when I say you're gorgeous with long red hair or this pixie-styled look."

Shannon met his gaze, more tears glistening in her eyes. "I've missed you so much, Jay."

"Same here." Jay hugged her, smiling as she squeezed him back.

"I-I still can't believe you're here."

"I never should've left your side." Jay kissed her temple. "I'm so sorry."

"I pushed you away." Shannon stifled a yawn. "I-It's not your fault."

"Well, I'm not going anywhere now, no matter what you say." Jay frowned as he looked at her. "You're exhausted. You need to rest."

"I don't want miss a moment with you."

"You won't." Jay scooted forward in the chair then got up with her still in his arms. He walked toward the hallway leading to the back of her home. "Where's your bedroom?"

"First door on the right." Shannon sighed against his arm as he entered the room and set her on her feet.

Jay gathered up the decorative teal pillows on top of her fluffy white comforter before pulling it back. He beckoned for Shannon to come over, noticing for the first time the lovely nightie she had on. Jay ignored the rush of desire awakening his cock, knowing the last thing Shannon needed was sex. He watched her pad over to the bed and flop back on the sheets with another weary sigh. "There. You sleep. I'll be here when you wake up." Jay started to pull the comforter over Shannon who groaned in protest.

"I'm not ready to go to sleep, Jay."

Jay stared down at her, trying not to look at her now hardened nipples pushing against the soft fabric of her negligée. "How about a massage first?"

"Mmm...that would be nice." Shannon barely covered another yawn. "I have some massage oil in the bathroom in the linen closet by the shower."

"Okay." Jay strode into the modern bathroom, went over to the closet and searched through the various feminine beauty products until he saw a bottle of sweet almond oil. He walked back into Shannon's bedroom to see she'd stripped. "Shannon..."

"What?" She shifted her long legs on the sheets, giving him a perfect view of her trimmed pussy. "Don't you want me?"

Jay came over to the bed, his cock thickened as he gazed down at her naked body. "You know I do, but not now." He shifted his eyes from hers to her rock-hard nipples then to red scar marring her smooth skin.

Shannon moved to cover her breasts as she turned her face from his. "I know...no longer perfect."

Jay sat on the bed beside her. He set the massage oil on her nightstand then gently pulled her hands away from her chest. "Shannon, look at me." Jay waited for her to slowly comply. "Nothing and no one is perfect, but you are perfect for me." He reached up to brush away the tear sliding down her cheek. Jay moved off the bed and got on his knees next to the mattress. He leaned over and gently pressed a kiss to the healing incision on the side of her breast, feeling Shannon tremble beneath him before he straightened.

"Oh, Jay." Her voice wobbled as she said his name.

Jay bent his head to kiss her lips, reverently moving his mouth over hers. The need to ravish her made him pull back just as Shannon started to wrap her arms around his neck. He chuckled when she groaned, reluctantly releasing her hold on him. "I want you to relax, okay?"

"Impossible when you touch me."

Jay grinned. "We'll see." He reached for the oil and twisted off the cap.

"Shouldn't you get out of your clothes?" Shannon gave him a small saucy smile. "I mean, if you get oil on them..."

"You're right." Jay stood, placing the opened bottle back on her nightstand. Beneath Shannon's steady gaze, he removed his yellow shirt then unbuttoned and unzipped his black jeans. Jay slipped out of them, aware of Shannon's sharp intake of breath when she caught sight of his hard-on through his boxers. The desire sparking life into her green eyes almost tempted him to fully strip. He had no plans to take Shannon tonight but hungered to feel her body pressed against his with no barriers. "I don't care if I get oil on my underwear." Jay winked at Shannon, grabbed the oil then moved to straddle her leg on the bed. He took care not to put any of his weight on her. "I'm going to drizzle a little on you, okay?"

Shannon nodded watching him beneath hooded eyes, inhaling as he followed through with what he'd said, trickling some of the fragrant liquid between her breasts. Jay poured more of the oil in his hands, wanting to do nothing more than toy with her erect nipples. He tightened his jaw, his resolve tested as Shannon trailed her fingers over his thigh to caress his stiff cock through his shorts.

"God, I've missed this." She gave his dick a little squeeze then let go, much to Jay's relief and disappointment.

"All yours when you're ready, and that's not tonight." Jay rubbed his hands together to warm the oil then smoothed them over Shannon's shoulders and arms. He kept his touch light as he worked the oil into her skin. "Close your eyes." Shannon obeyed with a tiny moan as he swirled his fingers in the oil between her breasts and tenderly massaged them.

"Jay…"

"Shh." Jay skated his thumb over her scar then brushed his slippery palms over her nipples, reveling in the flush of arousal sweeping over Shannon's skin. He shifted his body then massaged her stomach in a circular pattern around her belly button. Jay tried to ignore his rock-hard cock as Shannon wriggled beneath him. He caressed her hips and wondered if her need could possibly match his when she put her fingers on top of his.

Shannon opened her eyes to look at him as she moved his hand between her legs. "Please, Jay."

Those two words made him want to ravish and fill her. Jay dipped his oil-slicked fingers between her pussy lips, tapped her clit, and Shannon moaned. Her wetness delighted him as he moved off her. He wouldn't take her but he would make her come.

"Please." Shannon parted her thighs, letting him see how wet she was as he continued to tease her engorged clit.

Her seductive plea made Jay's cock twitch. "Minx." Jay slipped a finger into her, holding back a groan when she tightened her pussy walls around the digit. He kept his palm in constant contact with her clit as he added another finger and began to stroke her. Shannon moaned and Jay moved his hand faster in response. Her breathless pants became unintelligible words of blissful encouragement. Jay arched his fingers within her and Shannon cried out as she climaxed. Pre-cum dampened Jay's boxers as Shannon's pussy walls fluttered around his fingers. He slowed his thrusts, gauging his pace by her breathing until he finally pulled his hand from between her thighs.

Jay kissed her knee then got up. He went into the bathroom, grabbed a towel then came back to Shannon. He sat next to her then gently rubbed the terry cloth on her drenched pussy, enjoying Shannon's incredulous expression as he finished his task.

"Thank you." Shannon's voice was barely a whisper as Jay got up and tossed the towel into the bathroom.

"Your pleasure is my pleasure." Jay flicked off the one lamp illuminating the room then walked back to the bed. "So, thank you." He lay down, pulled the comforter up over them then cradled Shannon's body to his. He grinned when she tried to snuggle even closer to him, amazed by how much he loved her. "Sleep now, Red."

"Mmm." Shannon exhaled as she interlaced her fingers with his resting on her belly. "I think I can now."

Jay savored the warmth of her body next to his as he listened to her breathing gradually slow. He smiled in the dark upon hearing Shannon's soft snores, finally allowing himself to relax enough and join his beloved in dreamland.

* * * *

Shannon stirred beneath the covers, reluctant to open her eyes. She sought out Jay's body heat then realized she was alone in her bed. Disappointed, Shannon opened her eyes and saw a note taped to the alarm clock on her nightstand. Sitting up, Shannon pulled the note off and smiled when she read Jay's promise of warm croissants and coffee. According to the arrival time he'd left her, she had about thirty minutes before he came back.

Feeling more energized than she had in weeks, Shannon got out of bed to shower. She went into the bathroom and turned on the water. Shannon hummed as she tested the warm stream. Seeing Jay had bolstered her spirits. She felt better, more hopeful as she stepped into the shower. Shannon didn't care if she was being selfish. She wanted Jay to stick around. She wanted to tell him how much she did need and love him. It didn't seem right not to, especially when he'd gone out of his way to show how much he cared.

Shannon knew he loved her, saw it in his warm brown eyes when he looked at her, felt it in the caress of his fingertips as he touched her. Jay would do anything he could to make her happy and she wanted to do the same. She intended to make up for how much she'd hurt him by pushing him away and lying about her true feelings.

Shannon exited the shower, towel dried off then went back into the bedroom. She selected a hunter green summer dress to wear, a little number she'd hesitated to put on in the past because of its plunging neckline. Today, she wanted the man she loved to see her in the outfit. Shannon pivoted in the mirror hanging by her closet. She frowned when she noticed how the once snug-fitting dress hung more loosely on her frame. Shannon studied her appearance then sighed, some of her happiness fading. She looked different.

How in the world could Jay still want her?

Nothing and no one is perfect but you are perfect for me.

Jay's words echoed in her mind, making Shannon smile again. She believed him. He always made her feel beautiful and she was convinced he was perfect for her. Curls of heat swirled up within Shannon as she recalled her erotic massage with Jay. He'd been so careful with her, so tender, and the fact that he'd denied his own obvious need endeared him to her even more.

A lack of sexual desire had been a concern of Shannon's since starting her treatments. It had been weeks since she'd even thought about sex, which wasn't the norm for her, but arousal had been instantaneous the moment Jay had caressed her.

Beneath his touch, she'd forgotten about everything else and had simply enjoyed being a woman with a man who knew exactly how to bring her the greatest pleasure. Shannon giggled, delighted by the fact that her sex drive could be sparked into high gear with Jay. She couldn't wait to see him because she hungered for more.

Knocking drew her attention from her reflection. Excited to see Jay, Shannon hurried to the door. She pulled it open then gasped in surprise. "Mother!" Shannon froze as Clarion's wide-eyed gaze drifted over her from head to toe. "Come in, please." Shannon let her mum pass, pivoting to face her as she shut the door. She braced herself for scathing remarks about her hair, stifling the urge to smooth the spiked tresses as Clarion stared at her.

"Mum—"

"S-Shannon, I know about the cancer. I'm so sorry." Her mother rushed forward and hugged her.

Stunned, there was a five-second delay before Shannon wrapped her arms around her mum. Clarion embraced her tighter and Shannon's vision blurred with tears as relief washed over her.

"I love you so much." Clarion's voice was wobbly against her ear. She moved back and the tear streaks on her otherwise perfectly made-up face moved Shannon.

"I love you too, Mum." Shannon cleared her throat, trying to swallow the lump lodged there.

"I *hate* that you felt you had to deal with all of this by yourself." Clarion sniffed. "I know I don't always say the right things to express how I feel." Her mum touched her heart. "I wish you could see into here, then you'd know how brave I think you are—how strong and beautiful."

Shannon hugged her mum again, overwhelmed with emotion. "Thank you. Hearing that from you means the world to me."

"I'm glad because *you* mean the world to me, Shannon."

Shannon couldn't respond as she dashed away the tears falling down her cheeks. She didn't resist when her mum hugged her again. "Thanks, Mum."

Clarion nodded, blinking back more tears as she moved to sit on a bar stool. "Tell me everything."

Shannon joined her at the counter, glad to finally be able to talk about her situation with her mum. She shared details about her diagnosis and treatment, feeling guilty about not disclosing what was going on with her health-wise sooner. "I'm sorry I didn't tell you. I was going to."

Clarion gave her a bright smile. "It's okay. I know I don't make it easy to tell me anything. When I found out about your cancer" — Clarion shook her head — "all I could think about was possibly losing you —"

"Mum, my doctor's hopeful I will make a full recovery. I'm going to fight and beat this thing."

"I believe you will." Clarion dropped her gaze from Shannon's. "You *have* to, because all I kept thinking about too was how little time I've spent lately with the most precious person in my life."

"Aww." Shannon stared at her mum, shocked again by her words.

"It's true." Clarion looked at her. "Shannon, I want us to be closer."

"I want that too."

"Good." Clarion reached out to touch her hand. "And I'm willing to change to make it happen."

"Change?"

"You know" — Clarion shrugged — "soften some of my abrasive nature."

Shannon chuckled, pleased her mum even admitted to being abrasive. "*Really?*"

"Really. I know you don't believe me, but you'll see." Clarion giggled, lightening the mood between them. "Now, tell me honestly. How are you feeling?"

"Better." Shannon smiled thinking of Jay.

"Something else I have to thank Jay for, I'm sure."

"He should be back soon." Shannon raised an eyebrow, speculating over what else her mum had to thank Jay for. "Would you like to stay and join us?"

"Heavens no." Clarion gave her a knowing look as she got up from her chair. "I know he's bringing you breakfast and I'm sure you two have things to discuss. Let's do brunch anytime this week, if you're feeling up to it?"

"Okay." Shannon slipped off the barstool. "I'd like that."

"Me too." Her mother kissed her cheek then turned toward the door. "I'll call later to check on you."

Shannon followed her to the door and opened it. "Thanks, Mum."

Clarion's gaze was serious. "Promise me you won't decide to tackle any more life-changing events without telling me?"

Shannon nodded. "Promise."

"Thanks. Tell Jay I said *thank you* and I hope you know he's a keeper."

"I will, and I do know." Shannon laughed as Clarion winked at her. She waved to her mum before she disappeared out of view, descending the stairs.

Shannon exhaled as she shut her door then leaned against it, astonished and grateful by what had just transpired between them. It was a miracle. Shannon suspected Jay had had more than a little to do with it and she couldn't wait to thank him.

More knocking made Shannon pivot. She turned the handle, half-expecting to see her mum back for some reason but her heart skipped a beat when she laid eyes on Jay...minus his dreads. "Oh my God. Your hair!" Shannon yanked him inside. She circled him, gasping again as she took in his new do from all angles.

Jay rubbed his nearly bald head. "Do you like it?" He grinned, his handsome face alight with merriment. He sat down a bakery bag and two cups of coffee.

"I *love* it." Shannon shook her head. "But why? You loved your dreads."

"I did."

Shannon squealed as Jay grabbed her and wrapped his strong arms around her.

"But I wanted an outward show of my commitment to be with you through this. When you see me, I want you to know that while I may not understand everything you're having to deal with physically or emotionally, I *am* here for you." Jay caressed her face. "Mind, body and spirit."

"Jay, I love you." Shannon blinked back the fresh wave of tears threatening to fall as Jay frowned.

"You do?"

Shannon tightened her hold on him. "Of course. How could I not? I've never met a man more dedicated to my happiness." She laughed when Jay whirled her around then promptly kissed her. Shannon stretched up on her tiptoes to rub his hair, enjoying the way it felt beneath her fingers. Joy turned to passion as Jay cupped her bottom and nipped her neck.

"Say it again, Red."

Shannon moaned as Jay licked the area he'd just playful bitten. "I love you, Jay Dax. I love you and I want you...*now*." She pressed herself against his hard-on as Jay groaned.

"But—"

"No buts. I can have sex and I want it." Shannon wriggled against him. "Make love to me, please?"

Chapter Sixteen

"Gladly, Red." Jay followed Shannon into her bedroom, aroused further by her seductive laugh and the wiggle of her hips as she shimmied out of her dress. He stripped out of his clothes as Shannon sauntered naked over to her nightstand, captivating him with her beauty and strength.

She returned to him with a condom in hand, which he quickly donned as she got on the bed. The intense emotions flooding through him as Shannon beckoned him didn't compare to the first time she'd asked him to make love to her. Knowing she loved him and how much he loved her changed everything.

Rock hard, Jay moved between Shannon's legs. He kissed her pussy, enjoying her soft sighs as he began licking and flicking her clit. Jay increased the tempo and pressure of his mouth on her sensitive flesh when her sighs became throaty moans. He lapped at her juices as she dug her fingers into his scalp. Her little cry of pleasure as she came delighted him. He kept kissing her wet pussy until her breathy mewling abated somewhat, then he moved up over her.

Jay rubbed the head of his cock over her pussy lips before slowly guiding it a few inches into Shannon. She was so wet, so tight it took all of his self-control to pause when she gasped. "Are you all right?"

"Y-Yes. Don't stop."

Jay groaned with need when Shannon briefly tightened the walls of her pussy around his cock.

"*Please* don't stop."

Jay gave her a little more of him, delivering nice and easy strokes. He kissed her, taking care not to move to fast or go to deep within her. Jay savored every exquisite sensation washing over him. He worked himself in and out of Shannon at a delicious but maddeningly languid pace, until they were both breathless and sweaty.

"More."

Jay looked into Shannon's eyes, saw the need shimmering in the emerald depths but still hesitated.

"Please, Jay. It's all right."

Jay couldn't deny her. He gave her what she wanted, holding nothing back. Jay thrust faster and deeper. Shannon's sharp cries of bliss made him harder. The intoxicating erotic friction enveloped all of his senses, crashing over him in mind-numbing waves of bliss as he climaxed. Jay kissed her when he finally stopped moving within her. He slipped from Shannon's trembling body then moved next to her as she curled up close with her back to him. "Are you okay?"

"Mmm...better than okay. Thank you."

"You're welcome." Jay smiled against her hair. "I told you your pleasure is mine."

Shannon giggled. "Yes, you did."

"Do you believe me?"

Shannon shifted her body to meet his gaze. "One hundred percent." She tapped her finger on his chest.

"My mum stopped by. You told her about my cancer?"

Jay nodded, wishing he'd had a chance to tell her he'd spoken to Clarion before now. "Yes. I'm sorry. I didn't intend on being the one to drop that bombshell but she refused to give me your address otherwise. I hope you can forgive me for breaking your confidence."

Shannon smiled. "You are more than forgiven. She told me to tell you 'thank you'."

"Wow." Jay chuckled. "I didn't expect gratitude."

"I don't know *what* you said to my mum but *I'm* grateful." Shannon blew out a breath. "It seems like she's turned a completely different leaf where I'm concerned."

Jay grinned. "Glad to hear it. I just tried to impart to her the value of what's left unsaid between loved ones."

"Mmm..." Shannon leaned over to press a kiss on his chest.

"Speaking of which... You deliberately pushed me away in Vegas, didn't you?"

"I did." Shannon worried her bottom lip.

"You denied loving me."

Shannon dropped her face from his. "I did. I'm sorry."

"Why, Red?"

"I didn't want to be the reason you had to face cancer again." Shannon shuddered against him. "I was also scared."

"Of what?"

"Of believing in your love, letting myself love you back...only to be hurt or possibly rejected during the most vulnerable time in my life." Shannon looked at him. "Do you understand?"

"I do, but—"

"Jay"—Shannon grabbed his hand and placed it on her breast—"the reality is there's a chance I could lose this part of me."

Jay gently plucked her nipple. "I don't care. I'm in love with you, woman, not your breasts. There are options to explore together *if* that outcome happens."

"Seriously, Jay..." Shannon shivered when he skated his fingers over her other breast. "You want to love someone that could *die?*"

"Red"—Jay put his arm over her waist and caressed her back—"I could die too. I could fall on a pair of extra-long tongs or slip on a banana peel or—"

"Stop!" Shannon chuckled as she smacked his hand on her chest. "You're being silly. This is serious."

"Yes, this *is* serious." Jay brought his hand up to cradle her face. "Red, loving you is *my* choice, *my* decision...*marrying* you is my promise to continue doing so for as long as we both shall live and I don't care how much time that gives us. My soul purpose is to make you happy."

"Oh, Jay..." Shannon's voice trailed off as she stared into his eyes.

"So, what do you think?" Jay smiled at her as he brushed the lone tear slipping down her cheek. "Should we live and love life together?"

Shannon's laugh was infectious as she nodded. "Yes!"

About the Author

Nichelle Gregory has been in love with books and writing since middle school. A lover of the arts, she enjoys anything that embraces the creative nature within us all. Bringing believable characters to life that thrill and excite her readers is a challenge that continues to push Nichelle. She loves creating stories involving super sexy alpha heroes with divine heroines in magical, exotic, and fantastic scenarios. So, go on… Indulge your secret fetishes and desires!

Nichelle Gregory loves to hear from readers. You can find her contact information, website and author biography at http://www.totallybound.com.

Totally Bound Publishing